More Critical Praise for Tim McLoughlin

for *Alcohol, Tobacco, and Firearms*

"Whether in fiction or nonfiction, Tim McLoughlin is an armed and dangerous judge of his own crimes and misdemeanors within the New York underworld. His stories are both tactile and ethereal, offering the square world a scuba dive into the depths of what we do."
—Kenji Jasper, author of *The House on Childress Street*

"Alcohol, Tobacco, and Firearms couldn't be more New York. Tim McLoughlin drops a ton of big-city knowledge and wisdom, rich in lived-in detail, with humor that's hard as the sidewalk."
—John Strausbaugh, author of *City of Sedition*

"In *Alcohol, Tobacco, and Firearms*, Tim McLoughlin's slice-of-life observations about the gritty despair and raw humanity of New York City capture the pain and promise of our beloved concrete jungle."
—Nelson George, author of *The Death of Rhythm & Blues*

for *Heart of the Old Country*

A selection of the Barnes & Noble
Discover Great New Writers program

"Tim McLoughlin writes about South Brooklyn with a fidelity to people and place reminiscent of James T. Farrell's *Studs Lonigan* and George Orwell's *Down and Out in Paris and London* . . . No voice in this symphony of a novel is more impressive than that of Mr. McLoughlin, a young writer with a rare gift for realism and empathy."
—Sidney Offit, author of *Memoir of the Bookie's Son*

"Part coming-of-age story, part thriller, it's got all the ingredients for what may be a whole new genre."
                                        —*Entertainment Weekly*

"Stolid suspense from the land of the wiseguys."
                                        —*Kirkus Reviews*

"Sweet, sardonic, and by turns hilarious and tragic."
                                        —*Publishers Weekly*

"Cracks with the authenticity that only a writer with the perfect ear can accomplish."   —Robert Leuci, author of *Blaze*

"Tim McLoughlin is a master storyteller in the tradition of such great New York City writers as Hubert Selby Jr. and Richard Price."
                        —Kaylie Jones, author of *The Anger Meridian*

"So eloquent in its portrayal of the territorial nature of the once booming outerborough organized crime industry, felled by waves of ethnic turnover and the fleeing of the powerful to the safe exile of Westchester and Jersey, *Heart of the Old Country* is a fascinating juxtaposition to the comparatively quaint culture portrayed in *The Sopranos*. This is the story of those left behind in the migration to suburbia; those still hustling for the unaccounted racketeering leftovers like pigeons scrambling for the discarded bread the bigger crows didn't see fit pursuing."   —*Aquarian Weekly*

"McLoughlin in his first novel easily ranks with Richard Price."
                                        —*Penthouse*

"[A] raw diamond of a novel about teenage years and living life on the low end of the Mob scale."   —*Bizarre*

Alcohol
Tobacco
and Firearms

Alcohol Tobacco and Firearms

STORIES AND ESSAYS

Tim McLoughlin

BROOKLYN, NEW YORK

Published by Akashic Books
All rights reserved
©2022 Tim McLoughlin

ISBN: 978-1-61775-984-0
Library of Congress Control Number: 2021935230
First printing

Akashic Books
Brooklyn, New York
Instagram: AkashicBooks
Twitter: AkashicBooks
Facebook: AkashicBooks
E-mail: info@akashicbooks.com
Website: www.akashicbooks.com

For Renette

Table of Contents

INTRODUCTION

At the end of the day I tell ghost stories. Whether I'm writing mysteries or humor, fiction or essays, I write about ghosts, people left so far behind that they move virtually unseen through today's city. They're wandering exiles, living in an endless drift expedition.

This is not nostalgia. Nostalgia is different. Nostalgia rolls in from the suburbs, vaguely sad, increasingly misremembering, and with a whiff of superiority for having fled to a better life. Nostalgia is the line outside Villabate Alba Bakery on Eighteenth Avenue in Bensonhurst during Christmas week, cars double-parked for two blocks with New Jersey and Pennsylvania plates. Nostalgia is the crowd at the Danish Athletic Club for the Saint Lucia celebration. Ghost stories are the club the rest of the year.

Ghost stories are those of people living in four-million-dollar brownstones with no mortgage because the house has been in the same family for generations, but the owners have to clip coupons for two-for-one Subway sandwich specials. They have tenants as old as they are, or older, sometimes also inherited, and paying less in rent than an indoor parking space in the neighborhood commands. They could sell and live like kings, these ghosts, but where? Why are they tethered to a particular place? What happened to them here that compels endurance? Bound by a feeling of helplessness and rage, they move through a world that on a good day has abandoned them, and on a bad day conspires to destroy them.

I cannot take a single step in this city without feeling the weight of ghosts, the dead ones and the ones that walk with us. Yet no place I know is more scornful of the past, less loyal and sentimental. It's all swift, vicious movement, march-or-die commerce and art. And here's the funny part: the ghosts wouldn't have it any other way. It's in the DNA of this love-hate relationship.

To live here, you are required to attend your own funeral. Repeatedly.

These pieces were written over a period of twenty years, and much has changed during that time in this march-or-die town and its environs. Rather than update them, I prefer to let the older ones stand as time capsules. The maharaja essay, for example, takes place largely at the Trump

Taj Mahal in Atlantic City, between 1999 and 2000, long before the casino failed and its owner graduated from local embarrassment to global nightmare.

As I gradually became aware that the stories and essays were taking on a narrative arc of their own, I started writing new ones to fill in the gaps. Half the pieces here were written for that purpose, and are appearing for the first time.

It's not all about the ghosts, I tell myself sometimes. A few of these essays are fairly lighthearted, and after all, my more recent writing is increasingly personal. Then I remember the underrated gambling movie *Rounders*, and its protagonist, Matt Damon's Mike McDermott. Early on, he says: "Listen, here's the thing. If you can't spot the sucker in your first half hour at the table, then you are the sucker."

It occurs to me now that if you're a guy who tells ghost stories, and you can't identify the ghost on your first pass, then you are the ghost.

Boo.

Tim McLoughlin
Brooklyn, New York

PART I

STORIES

WHEN ALL THIS WAS BAY RIDGE

Standing in church at my father's funeral, I thought about being arrested on the night of my seventeenth birthday. It had occurred in the train yard at Avenue X, in Coney Island. Me and Pancho and a kid named Freddie were working a three-car piece, the most ambitious I'd tried to that point, and more time-consuming than was judicious to spend trespassing on city property. Two Transit cops with German shepherds caught us in the middle of the second car. I dropped my aerosol can and took off, and was perhaps two hundred feet along the beginning of the trench that becomes the IRT line to the Bronx when I saw the hand. It was human, adult, and severed neatly, seemingly surgically, at the wrist. My first thought was that it looked bare without a watch. Then I made a whooping sound, trying to take in air, and turned and ran back toward the cops and their dogs.

At the Sixtieth Precinct, we three were ushered into a small cell. We sat for several hours, then the door opened and I was led out. My father was waiting in the main room, in front of the counter.

The desk sergeant, middle-aged, Black, and noticeably bored, looked up briefly. "Him?"

"Him," my father echoed, sounding defeated.

"Good night," the sergeant said.

My father took my arm and led me out of the precinct. As we cleared the door and stepped into the humid night, he turned to me and said, "This was it. Your one free ride. It doesn't happen again."

"What did it cost?" I asked. My father had retired from the police department years earlier, and I knew this had been expensive.

He shook his head. "This once, that's all."

I followed him to his car. "I have two friends in there."

"Fuck 'em. Spics. That's half your problem."

"What's the other half?"

"You have no common sense," he said, his voice rising in scale as it did in volume. By the time he reached a scream he sounded like a boy going through puberty. "What do you think you're doing out here? Crawling round in the dark with the niggers and the spics. Writing on trains like a hoodlum. Is this all you'll do?"

"It's not writing. It's drawing. Pictures."

"Same shit, defacing property, behaving like a punk. Where do you suppose it will lead?"

"I don't know. I haven't thought about it. You had your aimless time, when you got out of the service. You told me so. You bummed around for two years."

"I always worked."

"Part-time. Beer money. You were a roofer."

"Beer money was all I needed."

"Maybe it's all *I* need."

He shook his head slowly, and squinted, as though peering through the dirty windshield for an answer. "It was different. That was a long time ago. Back when all this was Bay Ridge. You could live like that then."

When all this was Bay Ridge. He was masterful, my father. He didn't say *when it was white*, or *when it was Irish*, or even the relatively tame *when it was safer*. No. When all this was Bay Ridge. As though it were an issue of geography. As though, somehow, the tectonic plate beneath Sunset Park had shifted, moving it physically to some other place.

I told him about seeing the hand.

"Did you tell the officers?"

"No."

"The people you were with?"

"No."

"Then don't worry about it. There's body parts all over this town. Saw enough in my day to put together a baseball team." He drove in silence for a few minutes, then nodded his head a couple of times, as though agreeing with a point made by some voice I couldn't hear. "You're going to college, you know," he said.

That was what I remembered at the funeral. Returning from the altar rail after receiving Communion, Pancho walked past me. He'd lost a great deal of weight since I'd last seen him, and I couldn't tell if he was sick or if it was just the drugs. His black suit hung on him in a way that emphasized his gaunt frame. He winked at me as he came around the casket in front of my pew, and flashed the mischievous smile that—when we were sixteen—got all the girls in his bed and all the guys agreeing to the stupidest and most dangerous stunts.

In my shirt pocket was a photograph of my father with a woman who was not my mother. The date on the back was five years ago. Their arms were around each other's waists and they smiled for the photographer. When we arrived at the cemetery, I pulled out the picture and looked at it for perhaps the fiftieth time since I'd first discovered it. There were no clues. The woman was young against my father, but not a girl. Forty, give or take a few years. I looked for any evidence in his expression that I was misreading their embrace, but even I couldn't summon the required naivete. My father's countenance was not what would be regarded as a poker face. He wasn't holding her as a friend, a friend's girl, or the prize at some retirement or bachelor party; he held her like a possession. Like he held his tools. Like he held my mother. The photo had been taken before my mother's death. I put it back.

I'd always found his plodding predictability and meticulous planning of insignificant events maddening. For the first time that I could recall, I was curious about some part of my father's life.

I walked from Green-Wood Cemetery directly to Olsen's bar, my father's watering hole, feeling that I needed to talk to the men who nearly lived there, but not looking forward to it. Aside from my father's wake the previous night, I hadn't seen them in years. They were all Irish. The Irish among them were perhaps the most Irish, but the Norwegians and the Danes were Irish too, as were the older Puerto Ricans. They had developed, over time, the stereotypical hooded gaze, the squared jaws set in grim defiance of whatever waited in the sobering daylight. To a man, they had that odd trait of the Gaelic heavy hitter, that—as they attained middle age—their faces increasingly began to resemble a woman's nipple.

The door to the bar was propped open, and the cool damp odor of stale beer washed over me before I entered. That smell has always reminded me of the Boy Scouts. Meetings were Thursday nights in the basement of Bethany Lutheran Church. When they were over, I had to pass Olsen's on my way home, and I usually stopped in to see my father. He'd buy me a couple glasses of beer—about all I could handle at thirteen—and leave with me after about an hour so we could walk home together.

From the inside looking out: Picture an embassy in a foreign country. A truly foreign country. Not a Western European ally, but a fundamentalist state perennially on the precipice of war. A fill-the-sandbags-and-wait-for-the-air-strike enclave. That was Olsen's, home to the last of the donkeys, the white dinosaurs of Sunset Park. A jukebox filled with Kirsty MacColl and the Clancy Brothers, and flyers tacked to the flaking walls advertising step-dancing classes, Gaelic lessons, and the memorial run to raise money for a scholarship in the name of a recently slain cop. Within three blocks of the front door you could attend a cockfight, buy crack, or pick up a streetwalker, but in Olsen's it was always 1965.

Upon entering the bar for the first time in several years, I found its pinched dimensions and dim lighting more oppressive, and less mysterious, than I had remembered. The row of ascetic faces, and the way all conversation trailed off at my entrance, put me in mind of the legendary blue wall of silence in the police department. It is no coincidence that the force has historically been predominantly Irish. The men in Olsen's would be pained to reveal their zip code to a stranger, and I wasn't sure if even they knew why.

The bar surface itself was more warped than I'd recalled. The mirrors had oxidized and the white tile floor had been torn up in spots and replaced with odd-shaped pieces of green linoleum. It was a neighborhood bar in a neighborhood where such establishments are not yet celebrated. If it had been located in my part of the East Village, it would have long since achieved cultural-landmark status. I'd been living in Manhattan for five years and still had not adjusted to the large number of people who moved here from other parts of the country and overlooked the spectacle of the city only to revere the mundane. One of my coworkers, herself a transplant, remarked that the coffee shop on my corner was *authentic*. In that they served coffee, I suppose she was correct.

I sat on an empty stool in the middle of the wavy bar and ordered a beer. I felt strangely nervous there without my father, like a child about to be caught doing something bad. Everyone knew me. Marty, the round-shouldered bartender, approached first, breaking the ice. He spoke around an enormous, soggy stub of a cigar, as he always did. And, as always, he seemed constantly annoyed by its presence in his mouth, as though he'd never smoked one before and was surprised to discover himself chewing on it.

"Daniel. It's good to see you. I'm sorry for your loss."

He extended one hand, and when I did the same, he grasped mine in both of his and held it for a moment. It must have been some sort of signal, because the rest of the relics in the place lurched toward me then, like some nursing-home theater guild performing *Night of the Living Dead*. They shook hands, engaged in awkward stiff hugs, and offered unintelligible condolences. Frank Sanchez, one of my father's closest friends, squeezed the back of my neck absently until I winced. I thanked them as best I could, and accepted the offers of free drinks.

Someone—I don't know who—thought it would be a good idea for me to have Jameson Irish whiskey, my father's drink. I'd never considered myself much of a drinker. I liked a couple of beers on a Friday night, and perhaps twice a year I would get drunk. I almost never drank hard liquor, but this crew was insistent, they were matching me shot for shot, and they were paying. It was the sort of thing my father would have been adamant about.

I began to reach for the photograph in my pocket several times and stopped. Finally I fished it out and showed it to the bartender. "Who is she, Marty?" I asked. "Any idea?"

The manner in which he pretended to scrutinize it told me that he recognized the woman immediately. He looked at the picture with a studied perplexity, as though he would have had trouble identifying my father.

"Wherever did you get such a thing?" he asked.

"I found it in the basement, by my father's shop."

"Ah. Just come across it by accident then."

The contempt in his voice seared through my whiskey glow and left me as sober as when I'd entered. He knew, and if he knew they all knew. And a decision had been reached to tell me nothing.

"Not by accident," I lied. "My father told me where it was and asked me to get it."

Our eyes met for a moment. "And did he say anything about it?" Marty asked. "Were there no instructions or suggestions?"

"He asked me to take care of it," I said evenly. "To make everything all right."

He nodded. "Makes good sense. That would be best served by letting the dead sleep, don't you think? Forget it, son, let it lie." He poured me another shot, sloppily, like the others, and resumed moving his towel over the bar, as though he could obliterate the mildewed stench of a thousand spilled drinks with a few swipes of the rag.

I drank the shot down quickly and my buzz returned in a rush. I hadn't been keeping track, but I realized that I'd had much more than what I was used to, and I was starting to feel dizzy. The rest of the men in the room looked the same as when I walked in, the same as when I was twelve. In the smoke-stained bar mirror I saw Frank Sanchez staring at me from a few stools away. He caught me looking and gestured for me to come down.

"Sit, Danny," he said when I got there. He was drinking boilermakers. Without asking, he ordered each of us another round. "What were you talking to Marty about?"

I handed Frank the picture. "I was asking who the woman is."

He looked at it and placed it on the bar. "Yeah? What'd he say?"

"He said to let it lie."

Frank snorted. "Typical donkey. Won't answer a straight question, but has all kinds of advice on what you should do."

From a distance in the dark bar, I would have said that Frank Sanchez hadn't changed much over the years, but I was close to him now, and I'd seen him only last night in the unforgiving fluorescent lighting of the funeral home. He'd been thin and handsome when I was a kid, with blue-black hair combed straight back, and the features and complexion of a Hollywood Indian in a John Wayne picture. He'd thickened in the middle over the years, though he still wasn't fat. His reddish-brown cheeks were illuminated by the road map of broken capillaries that seemed an entrance requirement for "regular" status at Olsen's. His hair was still shockingly dark, but now with a fake Jerry Lewis sheen and plenty of scalp showing through in the back. He was a retired homicide detective. His had been one of the first Hispanic families in this neighborhood. I knew he'd long ago moved to Fort Lee, New Jersey, though my father said that he was still in Olsen's every day.

Frank picked up the picture and looked at it again, then looked over at the two sloppy rows of bottles along the back-bar. The gaps for the speed rack looked like missing teeth.

"We're the same," he said. "Me and you."

"The same how?"

"We're on the outside, and we're always looking to be let in."

"I never gave a damn about being on the inside here, Frank."

He handed me the photo. "You do now."

He stood then, and walked stiffly back to the men's room. A couple of minutes later Marty appeared at my elbow, topped off my shot, and replaced Frank's.

"It's a funny thing about Francis," Marty said. "He's a spic who's always hated the spics. So he moves from a spic neighborhood to an all-white one, then has to watch as it turns spic. So now he's got to get in his car every day and drive back to his old all-spic neighborhood, just so he can drink with white men. It's made the man bitter. And"—he nodded toward the glasses—"he's in his cups tonight. Don't take the man too seriously."

Marty stopped talking and moved down the bar when Frank returned.

"What'd Darby O'Gill say to you?" he asked.

"He told me you were drunk," I said, "and that you didn't like spics."

Frank widened his eyes. "Coming out with revelations like that, is he? Hey, Martin," he yelled, "next time I piss, tell him JFK's been shot!" He drained his whiskey, took a sip of beer, and turned his attention back to me. "Listen. Early on, when I first started on the job—years back, I'm talking—there was almost no spades in the department; even less spics. I was the only spic in my precinct, only one I knew of in Brooklyn. I worked in the Seven-One, Crown

Heights. Did five years there, but this must've been my first year or so.

"I was sitting upstairs in the squad room typing attendance reports. Manual typewriters back then. I was good too, fifty or sixty words a minute—don't forget, English ain't my first language. See, I learned the forms. The key is knowin' the forms, where to plug in the fucking numbers. You could type two hundred words a minute, but you don't know the forms, all them goddamn boxes, you're sitting there all day.

"So I'm typing these reports—only uniform in a room full of bulls, only spic in a room full of harps—when they bring in the drunk."

Frank paused to order another shot, and Marty brought one for me too. I was hungry and really needed to step outside for some air, but I wanted to hear Frank's story. I did want to know how he thought we were similar, and I hoped he would talk about the photo. He turned his face to the ceiling and opened his mouth like a child catching rain, then poured the booze smoothly down his throat.

"You gotta remember," he continued, "Crown Heights was still mostly white back then, white civilians, white skells. The drunk is just another mick with a skinful. But what an obnoxious cocksucker. And loud.

"Man who brought him in is another uniform, almost new as me. He throws him in the cage and takes the desk next to mine to type his report. Only this guy can't type, you can see he's gonna be there all day. Takes him ten minutes to get the paper straight in the damn machine. And all this time the goddamn drunk is yelling at the top of his lungs down the length of the squad room. You can see the bulls are gettin' annoyed. Everybody tells him to shut up, but he keeps on, mostly just abusing the poor fuck that brought him in, who's still struggling with the report, his fingers all smudged with ink from the ribbons.

"On and on he goes: 'Your mother blows sailors . . . Your wife fucks dogs . . . You're all queers, every one of you.' Like that. But I mean, really, it don't end, it's like he never gets tired.

"So the guy who locked him up gets him outa the cage and walks him across the room. Over in the corner they got one of these steam pipes, just a vertical pipe, no radiator or nothing. Hot as a motherfucker. So he cuffs the drunk's hands around the pipe, so now the drunk's gotta stand like this"—Frank formed a huge circle with his arms, as if he were hugging an invisible fat woman—"or else he gets burned. And just bein' that close to the heat, I mean, it's fuckin' awful. So the uniform walks away, figuring that'll shut the scumbag up, but it gets worse.

"Now, the bulls are all pissed at the uniform for not beatin' the drunk senseless before he brought him in, like any guy with a year on the street would know to do. The poor fuck is still typing the paperwork at about a word an hour, and the asshole is still at it: 'Your daughter fucks niggers. When I get out I'll look your wife up—again.' Then he looks straight at the uniform, and the uniform looks up. Their eyes lock for a minute. And the drunk says this: 'What's it feel like to know that every man in this room thinks you're an asshole?' Then the drunk is quiet and he smiles."

Marty returned then, and though I felt I was barely hanging on, I didn't dare speak to refuse the drink. Frank sat silently while Marty poured, and when he was done Frank stared at him until he walked away.

"After that," he went on in a low voice, "it was like slow motion. Like everything was happening underwater. The uniform stands up, takes his gun out, and points it at the drunk. The drunk never stops smiling. And then the uniform pulls the trigger, shoots him right in the face. The drunk's head, like, explodes, and he spins around the steam pipe—all the way—once, before he drops.

"For a second everything stops. It's just the echo and the smoke and blood on the wall and back window. Then, time speeds up again. The sergeant of detectives, a little leprechaun from the other side—must've bribed his way past the height requirement—jumps over his desk and grabs up a billy club. He lands next to the uniform, who's still holding the gun straight out, and he clubs him five or six times on the forearm, hard and fast, *whap-whap-whap*. The gun drops with the first hit but the leprechaun don't stop till the bone breaks. We all hear it snap.

"The uniform pulls his arm in and howls, and the sergeant throws the billy club down and screams at him: 'The next time . . . the next time, it'll be your head that he breaks before you were able to shoot him! Now get him off the pipe before there's burns on his body.' And he storms out of the room."

Frank drank the shot in front of him and finished his beer. I didn't move. He looked at me and smiled. "The whole squad room," he said, "jumped into action. Some guys uncuffed the drunk; I helped the uniform out. Got him to a hospital. Coupla guys got rags and a pail and started cleaning up.

"Now, think about that," Frank said, leaning in toward me and lowering his voice yet again. "I'm the only spic there. The only other uniform. There had to be ten bulls. But the sergeant, he didn't have to tell anybody what the plan was, or to keep their mouth shut, or any fucking thing. And there was no moment where anybody worried about me seeing it, being a spic. We all knew that coulda been any one of us. That's the most on-the-inside I ever felt. Department now, it's a fucking joke. Affirmative action, cultural-diversity training. And what've you got? Nobody trusts anybody. Guys afraid to trust their own partners." He was whispering and starting to slur his words.

I began to feel nauseated. It's a joke, I thought. A cop's made-up war story. "Frank, did the guy die?"

"Who?"

"The drunk. The man that got shot."

Frank looked confused, and a bit annoyed. "Of course he died."

"Did he die right away?"

"How the fuck should I know? They dragged him outa the room in like a minute."

"To a hospital?"

"Was a better world's all I'm saying. A better world. And you always gotta stay on the inside, don't drift, Danny. If you drift, nobody'll stick up for you."

Jesus, did he have a brogue? He certainly had picked up that lilt that my father's generation possessed. That half accent that the children of immigrants acquire in a ghetto. I had to get out of there. A few more minutes and I feared I'd start sounding like one of these tura-lura-lura mother-fuckers myself.

I stood, probably too quickly, and took hold of the bar to steady myself. "What about the picture, Frank?"

He handed it to me. "Martin is right," he said slowly, "let it lie. Why do you care who she was?"

"Who she *was*? I asked who she *is*. Is she dead, Frank? Is that what Marty meant by letting the dead rest?"

"Martin . . . Marty meant . . ."

"I'm right here, Francis," Marty said, "and I can speak for myself." He turned to me. "Francis has overindulged in a few jars. He'll nap in the back booth for a while and be right as rain for the ride home."

"Is that the way it happened, Frank? Exactly that way?"

Frank was smiling at his drink, looking dreamily at his better world. "Who owns memory?" he said.

"Good night, Daniel," Marty said. "It was good of you to stop in."

I didn't respond, just turned and slowly walked out. One or two guys gestured at me as I left, the rest seemed not to notice or care.

I removed the picture from my pocket again when I was outside, an action that had taken on a ritualistic feel, like making the sign of the cross. I did not look at it this time, but began tearing it in strips, lengthwise. Then I walked, and bent down at street corners, depositing each strip in a separate sewer along Fourth Avenue.

He'd told me that he'd broken his arm in a car accident, pursuing two Black kids who had robbed a jewelry store.

As I released the strips of paper through the sewer gratings, I thought of the hand in the subway tunnel, and my father's assertion that there were many body parts undoubtedly littering the less frequently traveled parts of the city. Arms, legs, heads, torsos; and perhaps all these bits of photo would find their way into disembodied hands. A dozen or more hands, each gripping a strip of photograph down in the wet slime under the street. Regaining a history, a past, that they lost when they were dismembered, making a connection that I never would.

SCARED RABBIT

"Okay, okay, so the mayor is looking to start a new antiterrorist task force and he only wants the cream of the crop from law enforcement."

Tommy Mulligan had settled into his joke-telling stance, his back to the bar, elbows resting on the hammered copper surface. He faced his audience, seven or eight other cops and a few nurses, standing in a loose semicircle at the back of the crowded room. Thursday was nurses' night at the Swamp Room, and the place was packed. Nurses' night at a cop bar was always busy. Nurses' night at a cop bar in New Orleans was very busy. Nurses' night at the Swamp Room was a zoo.

"Which mayor?" someone asked.

"What?" Tommy said.

"Which mayor?"

"Doesn't matter."

"Not this bald prick."

"Better than Barthelemy," another said.

"So's bin Laden."

"Could it be Morial?" a nurse from Touro suggested.

"Screw him too. All the money in heaven for Comstat, but splits hairs about the goddamn raises."

"It don't matter which mayor," Tommy said, sensing he was losing his audience. "It's a joke. Let me tell the fuckin' joke."

Tommy had been hitting it heavy for the last hour, and his face was already flushed and sweaty. He'd reached that point in the evening where he thought he was the wittiest son of a bitch on God's green earth, and that was usually Lew Haman's cue to leave. But Lew wasn't going anywhere quite yet. He sat silently next to Tommy, his back to the others, facing the bar in the rear, its rows of bottles decorated with casually tossed toy stethoscopes and white garters.

The Swamp Room had been a real bucket of blood when Lew was a kid, with a large, scratched, smoke-yellowed Plexiglas panel in the floor. Beneath it, two alligators were kept in a tank that, as he thought about it now as an adult for the first time, had to have been woefully small for them. His father would let him come in to watch them be fed, and more than the feeding itself he remembered the horrendous stench when the panel was lifted.

The space where the Plexiglas had been was covered

with stone tile now, and sometimes used as an impromptu tiny dance floor. The whole bar had been rehabbed about twenty years ago, just long enough that it was beginning to look shabby again.

"*So he calls in two state troopers,*" Tommy continued, "*two FBI agents, and two New Orleans detectives.*"

It was the awful end to an awful night, and Haman was not in the mood to indulge his partner's humor. He drained his Jameson on the rocks and signaled the bartender silently to bring another. *Seventeen years*, he thought. *Three to go.* For the thousandth time lately he lamented joining the force so late in life. He'd come on an old man of thirty and now felt like a dinosaur at forty-seven, old even for a detective; and fuck that television *Law & Order* bullshit with fifty-five-year-olds running down gangbangers in an alley. Everybody knew that if you hadn't secured a desk job, you were an asshole to stay on past your early- or midforties. You were an asshole or you were Lew Haman, with three years to go. Same thing, he decided.

"*So the mayor takes all six guys, and he drives them upstate, somewhere in the woods, middle of fuckin' nowhere. He tells them, 'Here's your first test. Go into the woods and find a rabbit. Bring it back out here.'*"

They had been only fifteen minutes from going off duty when they got the call. Lew had planned to go straight home after work, to skip the Swamp Room, the nurses, the drinking. He made such plans often, and rarely adhered to them, but you never knew. It might have happened tonight. Then the call came in.

Two uniforms had been driving along Magazine Street toward Jackson when a short, heavyset Hispanic woman stepped off the curb into traffic and waved them down. She told them that two kids had just robbed her on Constance Street. One held her face tightly scrunched in his hand while the other cut the shoulder strap on her bag with a large knife. The one holding her face pushed her backward unexpectedly, and she fell. Then they ran off, laughing.

The uniforms loaded her into the back of their car and started cruising the side streets. Within a few minutes she began screaming and gesturing at a kid in a hoodie and ghetto-slung pants walking up Fourth Street toward Laurel.

"That's him," she said. "The one that pushed my face."

The uniforms jumped out and confronted the kid, and he reached one hand under his sweatshirt. One of the cops yelled, "Drop the knife!" then fired three times.

So the first two guys to go in are the state troopers. They look at each other like—catch a rabbit, no fucking problem. These are Troop D guys, country boys. They go into the woods and they come back out in about five minutes with a goddamned rabbit. Mayor tells 'em good work and he sends in the second team, the FBI guys.

* * *

Ernie Lowell was about the nicest guy you could hope to meet. His nickname around the Sixth District was Reverend Ernie, bestowed upon him because he was always counseling fellow officers about staying on the straight and narrow, and avoiding the lure of drinking and dope, corruption, or ill-gotten pussy. He was married and had five children. To a lot of the other cops he seemed too good to be true, but Lew had always found him sincere. Though a year younger than Lew, he had been smart enough to come on earlier and was now in his twenty-fifth year, planning to retire in about six months. He'd never shown much interest in moving up in the ranks, and until tonight he had never, to Lew's knowledge, drawn his weapon from its holster, much less fired it at anyone.

Ernie's sergeant was the first to arrive after the shooting. He relieved Ernie of his gun and put him, shaking and in shock, in the backseat. Ernie's partner told the story to the sergeant, and the mugging victim backed it up. There were no other witnesses on the street. No one but Ernie had seen a knife.

Lew and Tommy arrived next. Lew dropped Tommy in front of the scene, then drove a few yards down the street until he could pull over to the curb. He walked back to Tommy and the sergeant. The kid in the hoodie was facedown at their feet, the hood of his dark green sweatshirt still covering the back of his head. There was a thin stream of blood running from under the body, and the slightest beginning of a damp red stain on the back of the sweat-shirt, as though one of Ernie's shots had almost, but not quite, gone through the body.

"What have we got?" Lew asked. The sergeant repeated Ernie's partner's story. Lew walked over to the partner and got it again from him, then spoke to the mugging victim, who also corroborated it.

"And you're sure this was one of the guys who robbed you?" Lew asked.

"That's him," she said, pointing to the body with her chin. "That's him."

Lew turned to leave.

"I think that's him," she said to his back.

"So the FBI guys, they take out an attaché case filled with all kinds of bells and whistles. First thing they do is divide the area into two sectors, and each one picks a sector. Then they disappear into the woods with global positioning equipment, sonar, and who the fuck knows what else. They're gone for about an hour, then they come back, and sure as shit they're carrying a rabbit."

Tommy and Lew stood over the body and compared notes as the ambulance arrived.

"Anybody else see the knife?" Tommy asked.

"No," Lew said. "Did you look at him yet?"

"Not yet. Shame it's Reverend Ernie."

"I know."

"At least Ernie's Black," Tommy said, and Lew looked at him. "You know, no media. Black cop, Black perp, offsetting minorities."

"No yardage gain?"

"Yeah."

Lew looked over at Reverend Ernie in the backseat of the sergeant's car and nodded to him. Ernie seemed confused, as though he didn't recognize him.

So now he sends in the last team, the New Orleans detectives, you know. Old-time guys, polyester pants and skinny ties. They disappear into the woods and nobody hears a thing for about three hours.

The bartender returned and stood in front of Lew. Lew looked at his glass and saw that it was empty again. How many was that? The bartender rapped his knuckles sharply on the bar twice, indicating that the next round was on the house. He gestured broadly at the row of bottles behind him. "Make a wish."

Lew looked at him and smiled for the first time that day. *Make a wish.*

He wished that his hands didn't shake so much in the morning. He wished that he didn't hurt all the time, like there was an animal dying inside him. He wished that his daughter wasn't living in Algiers with a drug dealer who might or might not be a member of the gang Lew just got

41

assigned to monitor. He wished that he wasn't having an affair with his doctor's receptionist. He wished his wife didn't know.

"Jameson," he said, still smiling. The bartender poured generously.

He wished he wasn't partnered with Tommy Mulligan. He wished he could still feel drunk when he drank, not just the dulling of pain. He wished that he hadn't stopped off tonight, or that he hadn't had this last drink, or that he wouldn't have the ones that would follow. He wished he wouldn't have to drive home tonight to Metairie as he did most nights, with his shield case open in his lap, badge and ID card readily visible for when he got pulled over. Mostly he wished he didn't have three years to go. Three years was too long. It was too damn long to be stuck with the likes of Tommy Mulligan, a bad drunk and a loud, stupid braggart. A man who couldn't hold his tongue for three years. A man who would crack if pushed, even slightly.

He wished he didn't make decisions that were wrong; knowing they were wrong, feeling compelled to make them anyway.

He wished there hadn't been three men on the scene before he arrived today, and he wished there hadn't been three knives under the body when he'd turned it over. Three knives stupidly, amateurishly tossed, practically on top of one another. He wished he didn't feel the sickening weight of two of the knives in his left pocket. He had left the one that most closely resembled Ernie's description. He wished he had six months to go, like Ernie, instead of three years. Three years if he could even get Tommy Mulligan past a grand jury without stepping on his own dick.

The bartender replaced Lew's drink again as Tommy turned and winked at him.

"So, after like three hours, there's suddenly all this fucking noise. Bang. Crash. Whap, whap, whap." Tommy emphasized every sound by pounding his hand—palm flat—on the bar. "The two New Orleans boys come out of the woods, and they're carrying this deer. And the deer is, like, all beat up. He's been worked over. So the deer looks at the mayor, and the deer says . . ." Tommy paused, savoring the moment. He was just telling a joke in a bar. Not a care in the world. He was beaming. "'Okay, okay, I'm a rabbit.'"

Lew raised his glass and let the laughter behind him blend in with the background bar din. It sounded distant, and somehow warm and cozy. Inviting. He wished he was there with everyone enjoying himself. He thought about where he'd toss the knives into the lake out at the West End tomorrow. He drank half his drink in a swallow and held the glass in front of him, looking through the amber fluid and ice at the bar mirror. Tommy Mulligan nudged him, hard, and some of the drink spilled from the glass and ran down his arm. He felt it inside his shirtsleeve.

"Get it?" Tommy said. "Do you get it? I'm a rabbit."

"Sure," Lew said, feeling the cold liquid almost to his elbow.

He continued to look through his trembling glass at the faraway party in the mirror.

"I get it," he said, "I'm a rabbit."

Seven Eleven

I was born on July 11 and have therefore assumed that I had no choice but to be a gambler. Although none of us asks to be born, and certainly not when or where, I believe my fate was further cemented by the fact that I was born in 1976, the year that gaming was legalized in Atlantic City. About a year after my birth, which occurred in Queens, a bus to Resorts International began stopping daily at our corner gas station. Back then the fare was ten dollars round trip, and upon arrival passengers were presented with a roll of quarters, making it a free ride. The quarters, of course, never left the boardwalk. My father enjoyed the slots and my mother loved the beach, so I grew up in the literal shadow of casinos. Sometimes these decisions are made for you.

Predetermination, superstition, and fate dictate the gambler's choices, and I am no exception. I'm not a stupid man, and am fully aware of the perception of foolishness attributed to an emotional investment in games, but in the larger picture, don't we all celebrate the random nature of the universe? We fear hurricanes and heart attacks, revel in unexpected pregnancies and promotions. I'm everyman, but more so. I am simply honest about my reliance on the vagaries of chance.

I might have been the CEO of a huge corporate empire if the winds of luck had blown my way. They did not, and that is why, at present, I am homeless and contemplating the robbery of an armed and somewhat vicious man. I have been standing in the parking lot of the Wantagh station, across the street from his bar, for some time now, and I weigh the odds of my success every few minutes. They are not good.

Wantagh has, to my way of thinking, always been a place where people go to die. Its population has grown dramatically in my lifetime, and Jones Beach has gone from bucolic to nightmarish, but it is still essentially the elephant's graveyard of the lower middle class. When I was a child my family referred reverentially to the enclaves of Nassau County. These were the towns to which my parents' childhood friends from years past had fled, abandoning New York's outer boroughs and scattering to the suburban winds in the white flight of the 1960s. It wasn't until decades later that my mother and father left their deteriorating neighborhood and joined them, everyone reuniting in geriatric, single-level bliss.

My father died, and that occasioned my first visit as an adult. My parents had been living in Wantagh for six years at that point, but I'd gone to college in California and decided to settle on the West Coast. I hadn't been back for a while.

I worked in the world of finance then, but repeated the same unfortunate scenario in every firm at which I was employed. I always exhibited great promise and remarkable early success, but my investment strategies would become increasingly volatile, and finally, when the risks had become enormous, some decision would not pay off, with dire consequences for the firm, and I would be let go. After three such incidents, I was barred from the industry.

Now it is my mother's death that has brought me back, though I would have been better served following my instincts and remaining in San Diego, where the climate is reasonably suited to outdoor living. But I knew my mother had a will, and as my sister had been killed in an automobile accident when I was still an infant, I was the sole heir. Or so I'd assumed. There was certainly no estate to speak of, but my parents' meager ranch on White Birch Lane would sell quickly and generate enough income that I might have a comfortable winter. And if I could double or even triple it quickly, who knew where it might lead?

I had not counted on my mother's increased devotion to Catholicism following my father's death. That, and the fact that I'd only contacted her once in the past four years—

to request money—led her to bequeath the house and her modest savings to Saint Frances de Chantal Church. So here I stand.

I was married once, and had a son. That was probably my grandest effort at integrating myself into mainstream life, but it was ultimately futile. I could not maintain with any regularity the mundane jobs necessary to support a family; and sex, with women or men, was really only a pale distraction from gambling.

My wife remarried after our divorce. A large, stupid man with a quick temper. He sold quantities of steel pipe to other large, stupid men. One night he got more drunk than usual and began beating her with a piece of pipe that he carried in his sales kit. When my son—who was six years old—attempted to protect his mother, her husband struck him in the face with the pipe, killing him. The director of the funeral home apologized to me for not being able to make his body presentable enough for an open-casket viewing.

My wife's husband was sentenced to fifteen years, and it seems he will have to serve eight. He has been in prison for four years now. When he is released, if I'm still alive, I will kill him.

Since our son's death, my wife has sustained herself with marijuana and wine. I attempted to do the same, but have found that neither drugs nor alcohol can cut through guilt and grief with the laser precision of gambling. It is only in those moments of action that I can still lose myself. That I can exist outside myself, in a world where my son is still alive, because my wife did not marry a brutal drunk, because she did not leave me, because I have no gambling problem.

This Sunday is Super Bowl Sunday, and for the first time in more years than I care to remember, I will be a winner. I will be a winner because I have an edge. Not an edge in the traditional sense, like receiving a beneficial point spread. This is more like inside information. It's like knowing that a key player has an undisclosed injury.

Suffice to say, my only interest in sports is a sporting one. That could broadly be said about my interest in almost everything, but with sports it defines a love-hate relationship. I find physical competition, between humans or animals, a pointless exercise unless the element of chance and risk of one's capital is inserted into the equation. There is no particular reason why any sane person should care, for example, who the fastest human being on the planet might be. If it were about traveling from one place to another as quickly as possible, wouldn't you simply take a taxi? Yet I have, on two different occasions, won five thousand dollars, and lost fifteen thousand, because of the results of competitions to determine that very fact on a given day.

My addiction requires that I process an endless flow of

information, from medical reports to pop-culture gossip, about people whose lives mean nothing to me and with whom I have no more interest in interacting socially than I would the horses on which I wager. I am like a Roman general preparing for a great battle. Every available scrap of knowledge is digested and analyzed, and at the last hour the most momentous, potentially devastating decisions are based on the reading of a bird's entrails. My life, and my decisions, have to this point been premised in almost as foolish a manner; intelligence perennially trumped by compulsion driven by blind faith. Until now. Now I have an edge.

My edge is this: I recently learned that the bar across the street is owned by one of the largest bookmakers in Wantagh, and that wagering this year—when the Giants are in contention—has been extraordinary. I have learned something else. The police will raid this establishment today, and they will arrest the bookmaker and all his employees. They will seize his gambling records and, of course, his cash. Unless I arrive first.

See, the money is gone, lost, though the bookmaker doesn't yet know it. So the question is, what becomes of it? The police will confiscate it and, after endless legal entanglements and court appearances, it will be forfeited by the bookmaker and dumped into the public coffers, where it will barely make a ripple. Or it will be pilfered by corrupt officers involved in the raid.

Or I will enter the bar in the next twenty minutes and take it.

I tend to be quiet around the police. No good can come from conversing with them at any length, and you inevitably give away more than you get. It's the nature of the interrogator, always taking it all in. I've been arrested over a dozen times, and though I've never gone to prison, I have spent more than a few nights in a precinct cell or backwater lockup. Mostly I pretend to be drunk. Police officers are used to people trying to deny that they are intoxicated, but rarely question your motives if you openly confess to being impaired. Since my arrests have generally been for gambling, or gambling-related offenses, being drunk in no way added to my potential punishment, and the ruse has often saved me from tedious and pointless questioning.

I have, as a side benefit, enjoyed the voyeuristic pleasures of being the proverbial fly on the wall. I've always marveled at the intimacies cops casually share with their partners, but this last arrest was the only time I'd ever gleaned information that I could genuinely characterize as valuable.

Like any degenerate gambler worthy of the moniker, I've got a pocketful of gutter-to-penthouse-and-back-again stories for most of the places I've drifted through, but in Wantagh I know almost no one. No one to vouch for me if I were to try to peddle my information to the target of the raid, or his confederates, or, for that matter, his enemies.

Besides, the police had spoken about this raid with an enthusiasm for the project rarely seen in law enforcement outside of film or television. It was to be huge for this town, huge enough to engender excitement in civil servants, and I found that excitement contagious.

I've never taken anything in my life by force, be it money, property, or sex, but I realized that even if I had the contacts to initiate an exchange with the bookmaker, my remuneration would be, in the scheme of things, paltry. It would change my circumstances, of course, but for how long? All my life I've dreamed of the big hit, every gambler's white whale. Perhaps I never realized the form it would have to take.

I began to obsess about the robbery the way I usually fixate on a big game or race. It builds over time and you find yourself doing things to ensure your participation in the event while still telling yourself you probably won't follow through. In the weeks preceding the event you squirrel away funds, or borrow them, or sell your wife's jewelry, or refinance your home, just to be ready. You probably won't do anything, but you have to be ready. And then on the eve of the game there comes a sign, an undeniable omen that moves you forward and places the bet. Sometimes these decisions are made for you.

This idea, this robbery, has taken on that feel. I have been moving about in a bubble, voices around me indistinct and muffled. I have convinced a social worker at SNG on Park Avenue that I'm a recovering heroin addict from New York, and she has enrolled me in a daily methadone maintenance program. I have been selling the methadone to supplement the money I've earned by cleaning the kitchen and bathrooms of a café in the Cherrywood Shopping Center. Sometimes they feed me, though they are not as generous as one might hope.

It took me only three weeks to accumulate the funds to buy the gun. Three weeks of living single-mindedly, obsessively, telling myself the whole time that I almost certainly won't do this. I won't commit this robbery in a town where no one left alive knows me. Where I gave the police a false name, and the charge was too insignificant to warrant fingerprinting. A town from which I can virtually vanish. I probably won't do this.

As in any high-stakes game, the clock dictates the risk level, and my situation proves the rule. I had been staying in my parents' house until last week, when the church engaged a real-estate agency to sell the property. They did not respond to being passively ignored with the same patience granted me by the clergy, and they changed the locks while I was out. Since winter has been thus far fortuitously mild and I still had access to the garage, I was able to sleep in an enclosed space and continue using my mother's lumbering Crown Victoria, so long as I kept out of sight and maintained the odd hours that, frankly, have always suited me.

When I returned last night from my trip to New York City to acquire the firearm, my mother's car was missing from the parking lot of the railroad station.

There are about a dozen taverns and clubs huddled around Wantagh station, born of an era that dictated that the suburban response to urban stress should be alcohol consumption followed by driving home. Though that attitude is presently frowned upon, the establishments have rooted deeply and continue to thrive in the new culture of designated drivers and taxis.

I had no designated driver, and though my cash might cover cab fare, I did not need a witness to my breaking into the garage, so I walked the two miles to the house.

Being on foot alone at night, even in the overgrown suburbia of Wantagh, the feeling of isolation was overwhelming. This had been Jerusalem, my parents' promised land. They had traveled here as children, and told me stories of Victorian homes surrounded by forests and farms; a dozen streets laid out with tract housing, then a huge cornfield, then another tract. Friends and cousins with backyards, lawns, well water, and aboveground pools. Success.

I looked for this magic on my own childhood visits, but found only the used dreams that had been inherited by cops and plumbers, bus drivers and bank tellers. Those with the luxury to dream big had already rolled east. We went to down-at-the-heels bowling alleys and the drive-in at Westbury and breathed in the last wisps of the good life.

My mother and father were blind to that reality, and I realize now that blindness can be a blessing.

The garage felt vast and soulless without the car.
Whether it had been towed by the municipality for some
infraction, or seized by the now rightful owners, was ir-
relevant; it only served to up the ante on my increasingly
claustrophobic circumstances. This morning, after the first
truly cold night spent on a concrete floor, I walked the two
miles back. I have been standing here for several hours, and
the clock is about to run out.

Three unmarked vans will have left police headquarters a
few minutes ago. Soon they will park on the opposite corners from this establishment and discharge the officers who
will execute the raid. Soon. I have timed their arrival to cover
my escape, but the schedule has absolutely no flexibility.

The weapon stuck in my waistband feels very heavy,
and it digs into my empty stomach. I need to decide now. If
I misjudge this, I will not live to avenge my son.

There is a crushing moment of self-awareness that de-
scends upon me as I consider my next move. These instants
of vicious clarity are thankfully rare, but when they hit it
is with the brutal force of unfiltered truth, like visions of
dying alone that visit in the night.

It comes to me that it matters not a whit whether I am
successful. Wantagh is where my family goes to die. If I fail,
I will most likely die. But if I triumph, then what? If this day

results in my greatest score in a life spent chasing the great score, then what? I will be penniless in six months or less, living in a shelter, unclean, and again contemplating violence. And violence, by all reputable accounts, comes easier the second time around, and easier still thereafter. Whatever good comes into my life I will destroy. And if some all-powerful deity grants me a second chance, with full benefit of the memories of this life, I'll make short work of ruining that too. Because I am a monster. We are all monsters here. We sacrifice careers and relationships, the bonds of family. We sacrifice our sons. Nothing is left but need, ever growing.

The moment is paralyzing in its weight but mercifully brief. An old green Saturn sedan stops at the light in front of me, then turns. Its license plate is GSB117, and there is a Padres baseball cap sitting on the rear-window shelf. Now I am golden. GSB. Giants Super Bowl. 117. 711. Get it? I was living in San Diego.

I open my jacket, shake it once to billow it away from the outline of the gun, and walk quickly toward the bar's side door.

Sometimes these decisions are made for you.

Rubber Gun

The studio had always felt tight and dark when I'd lived there, claustrophobic, the sort of small that makes a pristine room look like a mess when you toss your keys on the narrow kitchen counter. But the girls who lived there now, though there were two of them, plus cats, had somehow arranged their possessions in a way that made the tiny space inviting. I scanned the room slowly, but could not account for any one grand gesture that moved the apartment in that direction. Such things would always be a mystery to me. Like speaking French, reading music, or understanding the internal combustion engine, it was, on some level, an act of faith. I didn't know how anyone could do it, but I knew they could and I could not. I didn't spend a lot of time agonizing about it; there was much to be done. I needed to feed the cats of course, but also ransack the medicine cabinet for

Vicodin and Percocet, and set up the police-call scanner to listen to the neighbors' telephone conversations. And, if possible, I wanted to be back home by ten o'clock because I hadn't been sleeping well lately.

Leslie had reiterated her old warning that I might not see the cats at all—it was possible that I'd only know their presence by the regularity of the food disappearing and the commensurate accrual of shit in the litter box—but as usual, the first night I arrived they were sitting on the floor just inside the door, staring at me as I entered as though they'd anticipated the moment. The male, an elderly Siamese, was standoffish but unafraid, and the kitten, a gray tabby girl, was positively insistent in her affection. I wondered why Leslie always assumed they would hide from me. It was either their nature (and I was somehow special) or more likely just another instance of Leslie inventing a reality and then making everyone around her live in it. It was this gift of hers, I felt, that allowed her to book a cruise to Alaska for herself and June, her terminally ill girlfriend, when neither of them were employed and they had already been forced to sell their one-bedroom co-op and move into my old studio rental.

I didn't miss the old building much, though it still felt more like home than my new place around the corner. The new apartment was larger and brighter, and the level of cleanliness was about the same. There was a different super, but as with the rest of Bay Ridge superintendents, he was

Albanian, spoke twenty words of English, kept to himself, and from the way he managed to make the most normal activities appear furtive, was probably undocumented.

I unpacked the scanner and set it up on a barstool in the same spot where I'd ultimately placed it when I lived there. I had been out of work with a line-of-duty injury for six months now, and it was my sergeant who'd first suggested the scanner when I complained of boredom after two weeks. I initially resisted, because I associated scanners with EMTs, volunteers, and other buffs.

"I know," he'd told me. "I thought the same thing, but it helped a lot when I was out. I mean, you're just going to get the local shit, precinct you live in. I'm out in Great Kills, fucking Hooterville. Still, you feel a little connected. And you'll be surprised by some of the weird shit in your own backyard."

Another week of Maury Povich and *Grand Theft Auto*, and I'd succumbed. At first I only turned it on in the afternoon, and it was in fact oddly comforting. Bay Ridge wasn't as quiet as Great Kills, but it was a world away from the Seventy-Fifth Precinct in East New York, where I'd worked for almost the entire eight years I'd been a cop. East New York, just about the ass end of Brooklyn, seemed to be, along with Brownsville, the only part of the borough to escape the tsunami of gentrification that had so jarringly altered every other neighborhood. It remained defiantly low rent and high crime. It was a busy precinct and I liked it. By contrast the calls in Bay Ridge were mundane. A lot of shoplifting and domestic violence, vandalism and nuisance rowdiness. In six months I'd heard only two squawks for shots fired, which I'd have caught in a week in the Seven-Five. Still, I enjoyed the familiar cadence of the dispatchers' detached voices. I'd lie on the sofa, drifting in and out of drugged sleep, pretending I was still in the game.

A few days after I first set the radio up, I was listening to a dispatcher trying to hail someone to respond to a street assault, when a loud voice broke in: *"He sounds like the kind of guy who doesn't give a shit,"* it said. *"He's gonna do his job and no more. We're still trying to grow this thing. I want him out. Get rid of him."*

Then abrupt silence, a loud burst of static, and back to the dispatcher, still trying to raise somebody and now beginning to sound frustrated. I slowly moved the bandwidth dial in an attempt to catch the voice that had broken in. No luck.

Two days later it happened again, during a lull of low fuzzy silence between calls. A woman's voice came into my apartment, more clear and aggressive than the scanned calls. She was complaining about a pizza being soggy, suggesting that the only way it could be that wet was if it had not been cooked sufficiently. This time I heard the response: a thickly accented male voice told her that he was from Sicily, had been making pizza for forty years, and that she could go fuck herself.

When the radio went silent I approached it. Not being technologically savvy—I don't know what prompted me to do this—I picked the unit up and walked it slowly around the apartment, as much as the electrical cord would allow. About three feet away I got the now shrieking woman back. I pulled a barstool over and set the unit down, and that was when the floodgates opened.

Out came the rest of the pizza lady's hysterical rant, then a short conversation in Chinese, followed by a gruff-sounding man accepting a two-hundred-dollar bet on the Jets game. I was hearing my neighbors' telephone conversations.

I'd been a cop long enough to know that none of us, not one human being, is normal. We all have our good times and our moments when the mask slips. I was going through a rough patch. I'd injured my back arresting a suspect who'd previously been caught driving without a license, and who subsequently failed to appear in court. Not exactly a threat to democracy. My partner and I pulled him over for running a red light on Euclid Avenue and discovered the open warrant when we ran his name. Braced with his hands against our car, he pushed back forcefully while I patted him down, knocking me to the pavement. My partner easily subdued and handcuffed him, but I couldn't get up. The fall caused two of my vertebrae to compress. The pain was worse than anything I'd previously experienced, and even now, after two surgeries and the placement of

61

four pins and a bracket along my spine, I was in constant discomfort.

Because my injury was a result of the suspect struggling instead of striking me, the ADA explained that the perp could only be charged with the misdemeanor of resisting arrest. There had been, after all, no assault. The suspect pleaded guilty to that misdemeanor, and his public defender managed to have the plea cover his suspended-license charge as well. He was sentenced to three years' probation, and two hundred dollars in penalties that were waived upon his assertion of indigence.

I, meanwhile, was out for half a year, and remained in limbo. The department maintained that I would never be fit to return to active duty, but that I was not sufficiently disabled to be pensioned out. They were waiting for an opening in a light-duty assignment, most likely vouchering evidence, working in the records room, or distributing ammunition at the qualification range at Rodman's Neck in the Bronx. Such assignments were generally referred to as "rubber gun" jobs, given to fuckups and drunks stripped of their firearms, whom the union managed to shelter. These would be my coworkers for the remainder of my career. There would no longer be any avenue of promotion. I had just turned thirty-three the week before my injury; with eight years in, I'd have to remain there for at least twelve years. Did I mention that I was going through a rough patch?

I liked to think that if my circumstances had been less depressing, if I'd been working, if I wasn't in constant pain, if my girlfriend had not recently left me, then perhaps I wouldn't have been so immediately swept up in the voyeuristic appeal of listening in on my neighbors, but who knows? Like my postsurgical dependence on painkillers, it may have been an addiction waiting for a trigger.

Whatever the explanation, I couldn't get enough. Within a week I knew that the woman in the apartment above was sleeping with the superintendent, the fireman on the fourth floor had a serious gambling problem, and someone, either the sixty-year-old widow who worked nights at Methodist Hospital or the housewife with the autistic kid down the hall, was a phone-sex dominatrix. Also, as a building, we consumed a staggering amount of takeout.

Oddly, when I moved to the new building three months later—a move suggested by the department shrink to improve my mood—the scanner was useless for picking up phone calls. It still performed its function of monitoring police squawk, but by that time I'd acquired the eavesdropping jones. And, I realized, not just any eavesdropping. I'd invested three months with my old neighbors and didn't want to abandon them to start over with strangers.

I turned the scanner on and left it to warm up. The Siamese disappeared as soon as the food was gone, but the kitten continued to aggressively buff my ankles like she was shining my shoes. It was as though she'd been alone for a month. Leslie and June had only been gone for two days of what was to be a three-week vacation.

June was in the final stages of lung cancer. Given that I was pretty friendly with both of them, I was bewildered at how close to the vest they played her illness, and for how long. I suppose it's about the same with most people. She looked normal until she didn't. She worked until she couldn't. They insisted everything would be fine until . . . actually, they were still insisting that everything was fine when they dropped off the keys the day before yesterday. An added bonus for me was that they both continually insisted that June didn't need the copious quantity of painkillers she was routinely prescribed. I sincerely hoped that was true, but given her increasingly skeletal appearance, it didn't seem possible. If, however, they had decided that their masks were to remain on, even in the privacy of their home, well, there was no rule saying I had to suffer along with them.

They had been traveling almost since they moved into my old place. Mostly short trips, and, I assumed, checking off some sort of bucket list. I was tapped to feed critters and water plants, and took it upon myself to raid the medicine cabinet as well. Either they were being truthful about June not needing the meds, or their physician was Timothy Leary. Their bathroom was awash with opioids. Like most thieves I began conservatively, skimming here and there. I was already double-dipping on scripts, using two doctors but only one shady pharmacist. He had begun crying about the police drug plan, and how close he was to getting seriously jammed up. I had to lean on him more than I wanted to, and as a concession I'd switched to paying cash for the second round of prescriptions. As with all addictions, my need again exceeded my supply in a surprisingly short period of time. Thankfully, before I had to contemplate less-than-savory means to feed the beast, Leslie and June set me to minding the candy store.

Let's be clear: these are smart women. I'm an addict and therefore dumber and more volatile than I realize. They knew pretty much my whole story, knew that I was in constant discomfort, and I'd even hinted at my dependence.

"Hey, if it takes away the pain and gets you through the night, then what the fuck," Leslie had said. She and June could put away the chardonnay, but I don't think Leslie ever dabbled in June's meds. And I assumed that they noted my pilferage and chalked it up to the cost of doing business with an addled cat sitter. I'd always tried to be moderate with their stash, but moderate was becoming a fairly useless term of late. Also, their trips until recently had been three or four days in duration. Now, with my dependence at its worst, I had access to their larder for three weeks.

The scanner hummed to life and hissed pleasantly. I swallowed four of June's Percocets with a glass of Diet Coke and sat down in front of the unit. When I'd first started using the scanner, all I was interested in were the police calls. Now, although they were still the overwhelming majority of the output, I found that they annoyed me. They were loud and clear and harsh, often cutting in on delicate, intimate conversations between friends and lovers. They were the rude drunks at the dinner party.

A few standard squawks came in. There was a domestic-violence call to the apartment of a couple with whom the local cops seemed familiar. They were treating it like a weekly event, and perhaps it was. There was a group of teenagers who ran out on the check at Circles Café on Ovington.

And then I heard Samantha's voice, shockingly clear, as though she were standing next to me in the apartment. She said, *"I'm really exhausted. Can you hold on a minute? I have to pee."*

Samantha was Asian, she was beautiful, and under the oddest of circumstances, she'd hooked up with me two months ago. She had not moved into the building until after I'd moved out, but, owing to my new career as a therapy human, I was doing my laundry in the basement of my old building one day when she walked in.

It was a fairly boilerplate New York City story, with a plot out of a bad porno. We introduced ourselves. I identified myself as the go-to cat sitter for lesbians, she said that she was taking graduate classes in nursing and working as a tour guide on haunted Brooklyn bus tours. She'd just come home from a friend's birthday party and was a little tipsy.

We chatted through the spin cycle, and while I loaded wet stuff into the dryers she went upstairs and brought down a bottle of wine.

This was where it got tricky. I was taking upward of twenty pills a day at this point. Both my doctors, not knowing about each other, and my grifter pharmacist, not knowing of the girls' stash, had all expressed their concern about my intake. I'd long since stopped thinking about getting clean, and now just dreamed of regular bowel movements. I'd had one that morning, which I believe added to my optimism and unusually outgoing social comportment. But wine? I was a moderate drinker, which meant a lightweight compared to most cops, but since the pills I'd knocked it off entirely. I was walking around so fucked up half the time that I'd begun marveling at accomplishments like successful trips to the grocery store, or getting my laundry done in my old laundry room. Now I was in that room, already doped to the gills and proud of myself for hiding it, about to add alcohol to the mix. Or not. I could always decline the drink.

But, of course, Samantha had opened the bottle in her apartment and brought down two glasses that she filled before I could protest. And who was I kidding anyway? I managed to be fairly conservative, drinking slowly while we talked, and consumed only a glass and a half from the bottle while Samantha finished it. I was definitely feeling the effect, and not sure how the mix was going to work out.

If I'd had any inkling that this was going to occur I might have gone a little easier on the pills that day, but in fact I'd overindulged, thinking I would be alone with the cats and celebrating another raid on the girls' stash.

"Look what we've done," she said in mock horror, waving the bottle.

"Not possible, must have a hole in the bottom," I said.

"Let's leave the clothes here. I have another one upstairs." She tossed the empty bottle in the trash bin and picked up her glass. I picked up mine and followed her, wildly excited but having to mentally chant *one foot in front of the other.*

We made it to her apartment, where she opened another bottle. I had a glass, she killed the rest, and by the time we were making out on her couch I realized that she was probably as high as I was. We got to the bed in tangled missteps and had half-clothed sex as though we were following an Arthur Murray dance diagram drawn for a mosh pit.

Later, when she was asleep, I realized that I couldn't trust myself to walk, and I eased my body onto the floor and crawled to the bathroom to urinate. I stayed there until I felt stable enough to attempt the return trip as a biped. A few hours later, I collected my things and left. Samantha was still sleeping, and I could see no socially smooth way of waking her. And to do what? Ask for her number now that we'd had sex? Tell her I'd call? I really wanted to do both, but thought that perhaps I was better off waiting until I was somewhat recovered.

The day after, I discovered that her number was unlisted, but it was easy to retrieve with a phone call and a favor from the precinct. I left her a message, and when she didn't respond, I left another two days later. A week after that, she called and I missed it. She left a message saying that she'd been busy and had relatives in from New Jersey. She said she'd call when they left. That was the last I'd heard from her.

I was half hoping to run into her in the old building again, but at the same time I was afraid that it would come off as some quasi-stalking thing, so I avoided walking past the place unless I was visiting Leslie and June.

"Can you hear me?" she asked.

"Yeah. You sound echoey. Where are you?" The other voice was also female, and sounded young. I sat perfectly still and realized that I was holding my breath. I was certain that if I moved or made any sound I would betray my presence, then smiled at how insane that was.

"I'm on the bowl," she said, giggling. *"It's porcelain echo. Old building, old bathrooms. Such a goddamn dump. I can't wait to move downtown."*

"How are you feeling?"

"Better," she said after a pause. *"A little better. But I'm peeing every ten minutes. And I just want to sleep."* Another pause. *"Thanks for coming with me."*

I moved my hand to the off switch, but didn't flip it.

"*Sure,*" her friend said. "*You gonna say anything?*"

"*To who? My mother? My brother? I just want to move before I run into him again.*"

"*I'm sorry.*"

"*All bad,*" she said. "*Irish cop, nursing school. Here three months and I'm a Bay Ridge cliché. My mother would kill me. And there's something creepy about him. Oily. I was all fucked up but I think he's a junkie.*"

I turned off the box.

After a long time I went into the bathroom and took another four Percocets. Then I returned to the sofa with two small amber prescription bottles from the medicine cabinet and placed them on the coffee table. I opened another Diet Coke. The pills were kicking in and my back stopped hurting. That familiar warmth moved down my body, from my chest to my groin and down my legs. It had always made me feel bulletproof, but not today. I felt like a machine shutting down. Not breaking, not out of fuel, just shutting down. I took a few more pills and spilled some on the table. I gathered up what I'd spilled and ate those too.

I don't mean shutting down in a bad way. Just an engine that's done its job and comes to rest. It had gotten dark outside while I sat there, and I didn't want to turn on any lights. I stretched out on the couch. I felt like I was in a sleeping bag, zipped up to my neck.

The outlines of the medicine bottles and the soda wavered like the distant skyline of a small city in the fog. Then a shadow moved and a soft weight settled on my chest. The tabby started pneumatically pumping her front feet into me and began emitting a gravelly purr, surprisingly deep for such a small creature. Insistent, demanding, priming a pump. The girls would be gone for three weeks. *That is a long time*, the pills said. *Cats need to be fed*, the pills said. *We'll always be here.*

I fell asleep like that, with the pills talking to me. They spoke in a low, comforting hiss, exhaling gently like the static from the scanner.

The Amnesty Box

Appearance is everything and I'm a fraud. If I were to tell you that I have been wounded twice by gunfire, once in combat, and once during my career in law enforcement, those facts, presented that way, would paint a certain picture in your mind. And of course, that's my intent.

The truth? I was a cook in the army and was hit by a stray round of friendly fire on New Year's Eve in Kuwait in 1992, well after hostilities had ceased. The bullet passed through my upper arm, doing remarkably little damage and procuring me a Purple Heart, a trip home, and an early discharge. In high school I'd shown quite a bit of promise playing basketball, but had no passion for the sport. My war injury successfully closed that door and allowed me to settle into the civil-service career I'd secretly desired. I knew I wasn't good enough to play ball professionally, and I would not have even been a college star, though I was adept enough that I probably could have maintained the athletic scholarship I'd been offered.

The Gulf War fortuitously began before I had to seriously consider higher education, and I jumped at military service. My father had worked for the Department of Motor Vehicles and my mother was a librarian; I learned at an early age that security was to be found by burrowing deep into the bosom of bureaucracy. The Gulf War seemed a conflict ready-made for me. I hadn't counted on being shot under the oddest circumstances, but it could not have worked out better if planned. I had no real permanent injury. I had a medal. I had a reason not to pursue a dream that I knew I could never have achieved. And it was all someone else's fault. I never met the guy who fired that round, but I owe him a drink, if not a car.

After that I moved vaguely, but consistently, in the direction that I wanted my life to take. Since mediocrity, although the final destination for most of us, is shunned as a goal, it's best to seem to navigate it accidentally.

I applied and tested for several state and federal jobs, finally accepting the position of postal police officer. After training, I was assigned to the main post office in Uniondale, Nassau County. Two years later, a coworker was cleaning his gun in the officers' locker room, in violation of safety regulations, when the weapon discharged. I was shot in the same arm, and to almost the same lack of effect, except that now there is a lingering numbness and a recurrent pins-and-needles sensation above my left elbow. I was promoted to lieutenant as a result of the incident, primarily because the officer who shot me was the son of the Bellerose Terrace district attorney and I declined to push for disciplinary action against him.

The truth? I never would have received that promotion otherwise.

The truth? I was cleaning my gun as well.

The truth? Here I stand: Decorated combat veteran. NBA hopeful whose dreams were shattered. Lieutenant in the federal criminal justice system.

Appearance is everything and I'm a fraud.

There is no such thing as an amnesty box.

From time to time in some of the post offices in large cities and their suburbs, the public may be subjected to being searched. Though it's done rarely unless there is some specific security concern, there are signs in every post office informing people that it might occur. In my building, we rolled the magnetometers out perhaps a half dozen times per year. Often it was a random decision by a supervisor. Sometimes we were overstaffed and needed to justify our numbers. At least once or twice it was just to test the equipment and make sure it still worked. Usually it occurred on a Friday. Monday through Wednesday we were genuinely busy; setting up the scanners and making people empty their pockets all morning would result in lines snaking outside the building, down the steps, and out into the street. We had learned that through unfortunate experience when we'd first obtained the units. Fridays, very few people wanted to be trapped in our marble mausoleum, especially in warm weather. By afternoon we had the place nearly to ourselves. So Friday was the day of choice to step up the fight against crime.

Friday was, of course, also the day of the week when all the uniforms went out after work for a few drinks before heading home. This would occasionally engender a dilemma. Posted signs notwithstanding, people don't expect to be searched in a post office the way they do at an airport or a courthouse. They don't think about it. They rarely prepare for it. They often regret that.

Although my employment benefits include overtime pay for processing arrests, no one wants to spend the evening at Central Booking on a Friday night in the summer. The public never seems to tip to it, but arrests on a grand scale bear little relation to crime statistics in any branch of law enforcement. Arrests go down on weekends, they go down in nice weather, they go down when they are inconvenient. Conversely, they spike shortly after Halloween and remain high through Thanksgiving, when overtime checks will arrive in time for Christmas shopping.

The amnesty box was my idea. It was a cardboard box lid, cut off with a razor by the proprietor of the newsstand in our lobby. He would discard a few of them every Monday after stocking his deliveries. I fished one from the trash, invented the name and made an eponymous sign, and we were in business, Friday nights our own again. The theory was simple. As someone approached the magnetometer, we would call out the litany of items that needed to be placed in the gray plastic baskets stacked on the table. Anything with a substantial amount of metal in it: coins, keys, wristwatch, belt buckle, etc. At the same time, we would tell them that they were entering a federal building, and if they attempted to do so with any contraband they'd be subject to arrest. If, however, they voluntarily placed the contraband in the amnesty box, the property would be confiscated but no criminal action would be initiated.

It was surprisingly effective. Even on slow days we would collect a couple small bags of weed and a few knives. How it did not occur to anyone that neither the plant matter of marijuana nor the small plastic bag in which it was stored would register in a gizmo designed to detect metal was beyond me, but seemingly intelligent people tossed it in the box every time we set up.

Most of the contraband was discarded at the end of the day, as we were always in a hurry to get a jump on happy hour, but occasionally something would come up that could not be ignored. Once it was a felony-weight foil of cocaine, once three poorly forged credit cards, once a Taser. In those instances, we arrested the individuals over their protests, read them their rights, and processed them. I recall standing next to the DA at the arraignment of one such defendant. When asked how he plead, he conferred briefly in whispers with his attorney, who finally addressed the court.

"Your Honor," the attorney said, "my client states that the narcotics were voluntarily deposited into an officially sanctioned 'amnesty box,' and he was assured that no action would be taken against him."

The judge chuckled and looked to me. "Officer?"

I answered truthfully: "Your Honor, there is no such thing as an amnesty box."

I find myself a widower at the surprisingly young age of forty-two. My wife died two months ago, of cancer. The type of cancer isn't important except to say that it could not be attributed to any vice or failing on her part. Other than that, the most definitive statement relating to her sickness was her gallows humor. When she'd inform people of her condition, her stock phrase was, "I've got cancer, and not the good kind."

By the time her illness was discovered, it was already terminal.

I did what I could. I took a six-month unpaid leave of absence to better care for her, although she only lived for four months. I made arrangements for our daughters, seven-year-old twins, to spend more time with my parents and my wife's sister so that we could try to manage their trauma and keep them on some kind of normalcy track in terms of school and social life. It was and remains a balancing act.

I researched her cancer on the Internet and bought books. We investigated various experimental treatments available here, and looked into some that would require travel overseas.

When, toward the very end, my wife was overcome with a renewed fervor for her childhood Catholicism, I took her to the shrine of Our Lady of Medjugorje, in Bosnia. She had selected that site based on a dream. Travel by that time was extremely difficult, and I was fortunate that a close friend of ours was a nurse who accompanied us and made the trip possible. But she just got sicker as we both knew she would, and by the time she was moved into hospice care at a beautiful, very rural facility in Suffolk County, she only lasted three days.

I was there when she died. We were alone.

She held my hand and said, "I can't believe all you've done for me." Then she looked at me and said, "It's all right. I forgive you."

She didn't speak after that, and passed away a few minutes later.

The truth? I did not wonder what she thought I needed to be forgiven for; I scrolled instead to three unconscionable acts I'd committed and wondered which she had discovered.

The truth? When she spoke those words, my very first

79

reaction was to scan the doorway to make sure no one else had heard.

The truth? The last word I uttered at my wife's closed coffin before it was lowered into the earth was "please."

Appearance is everything and I'm a fraud.

It was seven weeks to the day after my wife's death that we next set up the magnetometers. It was the Friday of my first week back at work, and I was still wrapped in that cocoon of grief where everyone's behavior appears solicitous to the point of obsequiousness. I was looking forward to going out later. I hoped that the familiar routine, the alcohol and the company, would restore some stability.

At home I was trying to step up to the plate a little bit more with my daughters, but realized I was woefully out of practice. Friends, family, and neighbors were still in vigil mode, so there was no shortage of childcare coverage or prepared food. The trade-off, of course, is that your life is not your own. You are a guest in your own house, never clear on the shifts and schedules of the revolving door of caregivers. They sit with you late into the night when you want to go to bed. They drink with you and serve up platitudes and pointless insights. One told me she understood what I was experiencing because her dog had recently died. One lectured that I should not deny my loneliness, then suggested we have sex. As I stared at her I realized that not only did I not know her name, I didn't know what her relationship was to my family. Was she a friend of my wife's? The wife of a friend? A new neighbor? I so longed to return to work.

That Friday was slow, so slow that we were close to wrapping up with no contributions to the amnesty box, when a little boy walked in with his mother. We were supposed to work only in teams, but it was four forty-five. I'd sent my partner upstairs to get changed, knowing that the doors were closing at five. The woman was thin, Black, in her early thirties, and scowling fiercely. She was in a hurry and I was clearly an obstacle. I got it. We were in fact closing in fifteen minutes and today was one of only a handful per year when her locomotive momentum would have been disrupted. She assessed the situation quickly, threw her jacket and purse into the basket, and strode through the machine.

The boy, I would have bet he was ten but later learned he was twelve, walked up to the machine behind his mother and stopped.

"Come on, come on!" she yelled.

He looked at me.

"Put anything made of metal in the basket, sport," I said.

He reached into his pants pocket and put a handful of change into the basket. Then he reached under his shirt and pulled out a .380 automatic pistol and tossed it into the box as well.

"Do I walk through now?" he asked.

Stupidly, my hand went to my gun. He'd obviously disarmed himself, but the gesture is fear and training and muscle memory. I didn't draw my weapon. Tunnel vision removed the woman from my world, and I focused on his hands while I slowly slid the box out of his reach and toward myself.

"What do you have there?" his mother asked from behind me.

"Stand back!" I shouted, so sharply that I surprised myself. She did, and remained silent. When I had the boy's gun in my hand, I took my other hand off my holster.

"Step through the machine," I told him. It was quicker and safer than frisking him with no backup. He stepped through and the unit remained silent. I could feel my breathing begin to normalize.

"Look at it," the woman said. "It's a toy."

It was not a toy, but at first I didn't know what it was. It was the size and shape and, more important, the weight of a real firearm. It looked real in every way. But when I moved to eject the magazine, the release button wasn't where it should be. I looked at the gun, closely for the first time, and saw that it was molded from one piece of metal. It really was a replica, with no moving parts. Every detail had been remarkably copied, down to the slight projection of the magazine butt and the yellowed front sight. Even high-end replicas like this were supposed to have a bright coloration on the front of the barrel, so that they would be less likely to be mistaken for the real thing. I could see where this one had been painted over.

"It's a toy," the woman said again. "His father gave it to him."

She still sounded exasperated, but a lot of the fire had gone out of her. I recognized this moment of cautious de-escalation. She was trying to assess how much trouble she might be in.

I tried to match her tone. "Why would you let him bring this here?"

"Didn't know he had it with him," she said, sighing. "He knows he's not supposed to take it outside. I didn't want him to have it."

"Well then, problem solved, because he's not getting it back. Bringing an imitation pistol in here is still a misdemeanor. I'm not locking you up and I'm not even writing you a summons, but you lose it. Do you realize what could happen to him with this in the street?"

"Because he's Black?" she said sarcastically.

"Yes," I said loudly. She took a step back. "Do you really need to hear that from me to know it's true?"

She looked around quickly, at anything other than me. Then she took the boy's hand and walked to the one open service window. The boy was lagging and looking at me over his shoulder as she pulled him.

My partner and two other officers came into the lobby

in civilian clothes, waved to me, and walked out the front door. They stood on the steps; two of them lit cigarettes. I picked up the replica again, marveling at its heft and the distribution of the weight. It felt exactly as though it held a full clip. It was a handsome piece, and I knew it had been expensive. I couldn't resist trying to jack the slide back, but of course it didn't yield.

The woman and the boy returned then. She'd lost all her steam now and looked exhausted. The boy had been crying.

"Officer," she said, "I wasn't able to mail my sister's package. We came down here for nothing. Can he please have his toy back?"

"Hell no. I still don't think you get it."

"I get it," she said.

My partner reappeared through the front door, held his arm straight out, and pointed at his wristwatch. Then he went back outside.

"His father is going to make my life miserable," she said. "Please. I won't ever let him take it outside."

One of the guys smoking on the steps was pressing his face against the glass and giving me the finger.

"Here," I said. "Put it in your bag. I'm giving it to *you*, not him. Don't let him have it until you get home. Don't let him take it outside. Don't even let him play with it if you're not around. And for Christ's sake, tell your husband that too."

"He's not my husband." She put the gun in her bag.

"Whatever."

I was running up the stairs to the locker room before they were out the door.

The truth? I never intended to turn the replica in, and had planned to take it home and keep it.

The truth? I had sex with the woman who advised me not to deny my loneliness, and never did determine who she was.

The truth? The alcohol wouldn't work, as it hadn't for a long time now, but that seemed like no reason to stop.

I'm sitting in a confessional at Saint Frances de Chantal Church in Wantagh. Confessions are heard starting at two p.m. on Saturdays. It's almost two now, but the church has been open since noon and I've been sitting here in the dark for nearly an hour. I'm still badly hung over from last night's first full bender since my wife's death. We were married in this church. Our girls were baptized here. This is where we held my wife's funeral. It feels right.

A man has just opened the door on the other side of this booth, has taken his seat. He slides open a wooden partition, leaving only a screen between us. Now he will ask me to enumerate my sins, and when I do, he will fix them, and make everything all right.

The truth? That little boy was twelve years old and his name was Dayron Brandt. He was small for his age.

The truth? His mother lied to me. She gave the gun back to him as soon as they were in their car. That was why, when they were stopped for speeding on Sunrise Highway, the Nassau County police officer screamed for him to drop the weapon, at the same time firing seven shots into the car through the driver's-side window. Six struck Dayron, killing him. The seventh passed through his mother's arm. It was all recorded on the officer's body cam. I know this because I saw it this morning, on Channel 12 News Long Island. His mother made a statement to the police that an officer at the Uniondale post office had just returned the imitation weapon to her son an hour before the incident.

I still can't stop thinking about the weight of the thing. I think about it as I feel the weight of my own Glock 19 in my right hand. I think about how real it looked, even though that slide would never move. The slide on my weapon moves smoothly and easily as I jack a round into the chamber. The priest must have heard the sound.

"Is there someone here?" he asks.

I think about how quiet the boy was. How polite.

"Are you here to confess?"

I don't know why I'm so focused on the weight of that thing. I've got the Glock in my right hand and a pint of Jameson in my left. Of course the Jameson keeps getting lighter.

"Are you drinking in there?" the priest asks.

I open my mouth to tell him, but then remain silent.

The truth? There is no such thing as an amnesty box.

INDIGENOUS

When I found my mother dead on the kitchen floor, the first thing I thought was how different everything would be if I hadn't gone back to get my handcuffs. Selfish, I know, but I hadn't had a roofing job in a month, and I'd broken another tooth last Thursday. I was hurting all the time and really missed having a dental plan.

She was halfway under the kitchen table, on her back. It seemed like she was looking out the window. She must have been up and about for a while when it happened. She had today's *Post* open on the table, and two cigarette butts lay in the ashtray, smoked so thoroughly to the filters that they looked like earplugs. One piece of dark toast remained on her plate, and I could smell the whiskey in the dregs of her tea. I'd had a rough night and slept late. If there had been anything to hear I hadn't heard it. I hoped there wasn't.

The day's mail was next to her plate, and I recognized the green ink on the return address of the windowpane envelope on top. I took her Social Security check and folded it and put it in my pocket. Julio would open the liquor store at noon and cash it, as he always did.

I looked around the room. I was born here forty years ago. I grew up here, then moved out and got a job and got married and got fired and got divorced and moved back. It seemed like there should be more to it than that, but really, there wasn't.

The small white octagonal floor tiles were identical to those in the bar at the Knights of Columbus on Van Brunt Street, where my parents held my christening party, and where I'd had my wedding reception. The Knights folded about six months ago, unable to keep up with the mounting rents in Red Hook. I would have to move now too. This lease was in my mother's name, and ours was the last rent-controlled apartment in the building. The landlord had already gotten most of the Blacks and Puerto Ricans and old Irish out and was stocking the place with yuppies. Manhattan people, we called them, or just "the new people."

I left then, went down three flights and hit the street and walked.

In the summer of 1997, I graduated from the police academy. That night, about a dozen of us wound up in Coney Island, pretty drunk by two in the morning. It seemed funny. I handcuffed the ride operator to his ticket booth and we hijacked the Wonder Wheel. We let the pretty girls ride free, and stopped and started it when we felt like it, and someone brought more beer. When they caught us there was a lot of press. Somebody had to swing. The rest of my friends almost had their twenty in now, and they were all living upstate or in Jersey. I'd gone back for my handcuffs.

I stepped into the new place where the Knights had been. It was unbearably bright. They'd just opened, and the only people there were the bartender and a couple having coffee at the bar. The room was newly painted and scrubbed clean and smelled of polyurethane instead of beer. I ordered a drink, and remembered standing outside with the old-timers a few years ago, laughing at the city road crew as they painted a double yellow line down the street for the first time.

"Where you from?" the bartender asked.

He was young and fit. He looked intelligent. He looked like he had sex with attractive women. He looked like he had a future. There must be a word, I thought; a way to tell him.

I was angry, suddenly. I wanted to smack him just for talking to me, just for being in this place. I wanted to smack him for the plants in the window and the missing jukebox and the flat-screen television and the six-dollar beer. And I felt ashamed. My mother was dead on the floor and I was back in a bar, and now I'd spent my last six dollars. My tongue kept cutting itself on the new broken tooth, and it hurt, and I felt like I couldn't talk.

"You okay, dude?" he asked.

"Standing still," I said.

"What?"

"Not moving."

I felt dizzy and the words weren't coming out right. I was starting to cry. I wiped my eyes and saw the thick black lines of grime under my fingernails and looked away, down at the polished wood floor where the white octagonal tiles had been. I thought about the Blacks and the Puerto Ricans and the Italians, and the fights and the parties, and how when we were kids we would play along the pier on the corner at Erie Basin, pretending we were Indians watching the first white men arrive. I was sobbing now and my head hurt. The couple with coffee was looking at me and I didn't care.

"From here!" I screamed. "From here!"

PART II
ESSAYS

RALPH AND SAM

When you carry a gun and a badge, people will sometimes pay you to rob other people. This is, of course, all perfectly legal. So it was that I found myself halfway down a dark entry ramp to an underground garage near Rockefeller Center, trying to take property from a gentleman intent on not parting with it. I'd chased him for two blocks, my partners trailing behind. When I finally confronted him and ordered him to give it up, he steeled himself for a fight, and I did too. Then my first partner arrived, and panting for breath behind him, my second accomplice. Our victim reassessed the situation quickly and decided that the fight was over. The guy I would later come to know as Dixie surrendered his loot, and we left him standing there cursing our mothers as we walked back up the ramp.

"How'd we do?" my regular partner, Lou, asked.

"Not great," I said as I shook out our bounty and separated it. I was holding two black Iron Maiden T-shirts, one sized small and one medium.

"Another opportunity around every corner," Lou said as we walked back toward Radio City Music Hall.

One of the first things I discovered when I began working as a court officer in New York City Criminal Court was that just about every one of my coworkers held down a second job. If you were able to legally carry a firearm in this town in the early 1980s, you were showered with employment opportunities, all in security work of some kind. I was twenty-five years old when I graduated from the academy and got assigned to Brooklyn Criminal, and up to that point all the jobs I'd had involved lifting heavy objects or driving. Suddenly, people were willing to pay me a great deal of money to stand around and do nothing.

It should be noted that, as with any well-paying stand-around job, the compensation generally reflects an obligation for the payee to deal with anything unpleasant, messy, or dangerous that may arise during those protracted periods of doing nothing. Just ask a firefighter.

During my first year, I had a half dozen part-time jobs. Some were one-offs, like personal security, being a bodyguard to someone passing through, or an armed chauffeur for people with too much money who wanted to be picked up and delivered back to their Westchester or Long Island enclaves. The easiest of these were theater gigs, because you dropped the rich people off, watched them enter the theater, then drove downtown and found a place to eat dinner. A couple of hours later you made certain to be outside when they emerged and took them home, having been on the clock for the entire evening.

I did bank drops for a few movie theaters, all-cash businesses back then. A busy theater in Manhattan on a Friday or Saturday night might have three such drops with fifteen to twenty thousand dollars each. Coney Island's rides, arcades, food stalls, and vendors were even busier. There was always work in the diamond district, hanging around upstairs offices on 47th Street, and occasionally walking one of the merchants to another establishment, or, more often, just to meet with a colleague on the busy Midtown sidewalk where envelopes containing diamonds, and sometimes cash, changed hands openly, but quickly and unobtrusively, amid the thrum of street chaos.

But among all the oddball off-the-books ways of supplementing my income, the one that I kept for the longest time, and ultimately enjoyed the most, was the T-shirt seizures.

I'd been working security at Radio City for a few months when the T-shirt job was proffered. Radio City Music Hall was a sweet if not particularly lucrative gig. You were indoors, wore a suit, and got to see a show. Most of the guys I worked with were older, usually in their forties and coasting the last few years to retirement. They wanted the easy money, which meant the easy shows. Concert geezer fests like Liberace, Julio Iglesias, and the six-week run of the Rockettes Christmas show were their bread and butter. I worked my share of those, but I also signed up for concerts that the older guys avoided because they were more hands-on in terms of crowd control and possible trouble. I worked shows like U2, Roger Waters, Third World, and the Cure that summer. It was while working backstage for Willie Nelson that I was approached for outside work.

The catering for Willie and his band was biblical in proportion, a twenty-foot spread consisting of all manner of Southern delicacies. The whole backstage area was redolent of smoked meat and sauces, beer and whiskey. It was like a huge country picnic in Midtown Manhattan. Those tasty victuals were strictly off-limits to the hired help, but I was drooling over them as I set my containers of Chinese takeout on the folding table by the 53rd Street stage door. Willie had passed by a few times, and we'd nodded and smiled at each other. The next time he passed, he stopped and looked at the table, then at me.

"Chinese food?" he asked.

"It is," I said.

"Man," he said, "I would kill for Chinese food."

Five minutes later I had a towering stack of ribs, greens, and corn on the cob, and Willie had my dinner. When the band took to the stage, I settled in to my feast, and in that moment, as happens to every human who has ever stretched a rule on a jobsite, my boss walked in.

The good news was that he didn't seem to give a damn about my infraction, if he noticed it. The better news was that he offered me a job making substantially more money beginning in a few days.

"Outdoor work. Trademark enforcement. No more monkey suit. You'll love it."

This was how, a week after swapping food with Willie Nelson, I found myself in a dark garage stealing Iron Maiden T-shirts.

Trademark enforcement. It was a new one on me, but if you're doing it right, all life is a learning curve. Apparently, once you copyright anything related to a brand, someone will try to steal it if it's worth stealing. The same way Chanel and Louis Vuitton and Rolex have to combat the knock-off market, performers are susceptible brands. Brands are copyrighted. Copyrights need to be protected or, past a point, they are deemed abandoned.

The nuance of copyright was not yet known to Dixie the first time I robbed him, but he was smarter than me, and ultimately made the connections before I did, which led to the arrangement making this the best side gig of my career.

The security company for which I worked had a contract to enforce the copyright of any artist performing at a venue they were protecting. This meant that anyone selling anything with the name or likeness of the artist or band, within ten blocks of the venue, was subject to having their property confiscated.

What made this legal was an order stating that it was legal, specific to a certain event, location and date, signed by a federal judge. Before embarking on our rounds, we were all given dozens of copies of this order. At the bottom of each copy was a box to fill in the quantity of the contraband seized, and a line to be initialed. Nobody bothered serving the orders, and the old-timers threw them away before they hit the street. It wasn't like we were keeping track of product. At the end of the night, the shirts were thrown in a pile in some small office and then sent out to be destroyed. Nobody was counting anything.

To prep me for the first night of work, my supervisor had told me that it was an Iron Maiden concert, and suggested that I look like someone attending the show. I had lost my ponytail the previous year before entering the court officer academy, but I spiked out what hair I had, put a gold hoop in my ear, and donned a black sleeveless Iggy Pop T-shirt that stated *Fun Can Kill* over Iggy's visage. With black jeans and Capezios I showed up outside Radio City and walked over to the twenty or so guys gathered by the stage door, most of whom I'd worked with before. I shouldered my way into the circle, and the boss looked at me then over me. He came back a moment later.

"Timmy?" he said. "Shit, you look great. This is what

I'm talking about, people. Someone will sell him a shirt."

The rest of our crew looked like off-duty cops. No, it was actually worse than that. They looked like off-duty cops trying to look like the cool parent chaperoning their kid's junior high dance. No, it was worse than that. Well, whatever. It was a Rockports and Dockers festival and they could not have pulled off selling weed to your grandmother at a Bob Weir show.

The premise was simple, the details you learned on the fly. Back then, licensed product averaged twenty-two dollars for a T-shirt in Radio City or Madison Square Garden. Bootleggers sold knockoff merch outside for ten dollars a pop. Our job was to make sure that concertgoers were only able to avail themselves of the sanctioned, expensive crap. I was partnered that night with my friend Lou, with whom I worked in the courthouse. Most of the teams were two guys, but because we were new they put us with an old-timer named Joe, an investigator for the DA's office. He was ten years older than us, twenty pounds heavier, bald, and a drunk. He made it clear to us that he had no intention of breaking a sweat, and that he saw our role to be a physical presence, to keep the illegal vendors at least across the avenue from the crowds.

While he was still talking, I saw Dixie out of the corner of my eye offering a shirt to two young girls near the entrance. I approached him, and while we haggled over the price, Joe waddled up.

"You can't sell those here," he bellowed. "Illegal merchandise. Give 'em to me."

Dixie took off, I pursued, and the rest was fate.

I learned a lot that first night. Mostly I learned that I didn't like Joe and that it would be wise to ignore his direction. Even with him as an anchor, we ended the night with about twenty bootleg shirts. The boss was thrilled, and Lou and I were able to shed Joe and work alone from then on.

We picked up a few important steps in the next few weeks. Number one among those was to make sure the police knew about us. When you're robbing citizens openly in the street, you don't want to be mistaken for someone robbing citizens openly in the street. At big venues like Madison Square Garden there was always a large police presence. There was a command vehicle, usually the size of a motor home, and thirty or forty uniforms attached. We would always begin the night by approaching the bus, flashing our shields to get in, and asking to speak to the lieutenant in charge. We'd let him know who we were and why we were there. Then of course we'd ask if he had any kids. He did, really? Are they into fill-in-the-blank? Great. We'll make sure we drop off a dozen or so shirts before we get out of here. Have a nice night.

There were two intensely busy periods of time during these gigs, separated by a long break. For most shows we arrived a couple of hours before the concert began, and worked until about an hour after it ended. The period after the show was known as "the blowout," because it was the last opportunity for the vendors to move their merch. The blowout could be fierce, especially on the last night of a three- or four-day stand. After that, the shirts were pretty much worthless to the vendors.

During the actual performance, there really wasn't anything to do. All the potential buyers were inside the venue. Outside became a ghost town surprisingly quickly, and we got an extended meal break.

Most of the older guys were drinkers, and while we were certainly on our way down that well-worn law enforcement path, we were naive enough not to do it on the clock yet, and young enough that we wanted to be able to chase the bootleg guys up and down the streets without being disadvantaged by three beers. The nights we worked the Garden, the old-timers spent their downtime in the Blarney Stone on Eighth Avenue, and my crew of a half dozen younger guys went to the McDonald's on Seventh.

What hadn't occurred to us was that the bootleggers were keeping the same hours that we were. The third or fourth show that we worked was at the Garden, and that was the first time we hit McDonald's. I paid for my food and carried my tray upstairs ahead of my friends to scout a table. That was when I saw the guy I had robbed a few weeks earlier outside Radio City, sitting with eight or nine of his young coworkers at three booths by the window.

Awkward isn't exactly the right word, but it will do.

We locked eyes, and I certainly hesitated, but the only free tables were right across from theirs. They were laughing and talking loudly, and there were an awful lot of shirts in open view, draped over tables and seats.

I walked over and sat, Dixie's eyes burning a hole in me. He didn't know I had friends joining me momentarily. No effort was made to conceal or safeguard any of the shirts. Dixie looked at me like I was something he'd stepped in.

"The fuck you doing here?" he said. The other guys got quiet.

I considered my answer for a moment, but came up blank. I shrugged. "Lunch break."

He looked at me incredulously. "Lunch break?"

I sat still, watching his hands, trying to keep everyone else in sight.

"Lunch break?" he said again. He stared at me for a few more seconds, and then said "Lunch break" a third time. Then he started laughing.

When he laughed, the rest of the young guys began to laugh. One waved a T-shirt at me like a toreador taunting a bull, but Dixie brushed him off.

"No no no," he said, smiling. "Lunch break."

A few of the other guys muttered "lunch break" and chuckled and cursed. One or two seemed unhappy, but it was pretty clear Dixie was in charge. He stiffened when my friends arrived, and we did the awkward moment again.

"Sit down," I told them. "Everything's cool. We're all on lunch."

That was how it started. We sat together during our meal breaks for almost every concert that I worked at the Garden thereafter.

There are several analogies for the social interaction that began to form between our groups. If I want to be high-minded, I can summon the reputed baseball game played during the Civil War between Stonewall Jackson's second brigade and an outfit of Union troops recounted in Wells Twombly's *200 Years of Sport in America*. I'm rarely feeling high-minded, however, and truth be told, we were all a lot more like Ralph and Sam, the wolf and sheepdog from Chuck Jones's series of Warner Bros. cartoons from the 1950s. We punched in, exchanged pleasantries, and began battling. At break time we ate together and chatted, then went outside and did it again. The question of who was the wolf and who the sheepdog merited consideration, but I surely wasn't about to be that honest with myself.

Those meal breaks ultimately changed everything. We learned a great deal from those kids, and about them. What they got from us, besides an occasional milkshake, I don't know, but they were more gracious than we deserved.

Dixie, as I've said, was the de facto leader. I never knew his real name, but his Southern accent made the sobriquet obvious. He learned our names and never forgot them or mixed us up. He never seemed to forget anything. His crew was young, Black, and all were American except for one Jamaican guy. They all lived within a few blocks of each other in Harlem. I never found out how they got the T-shirt gig, but I did take in a lot of information about it.

We'd always known there was a van, and that the van was headquarters on wheels for the bootleg vendors, but that was about all we knew.

From Dixie I learned that the van came in from Jersey City, and that a pair of Italian cousins drove it in for the shows. It was loaded with contraband nearly to the roof, around a thousand shirts. Each kid was given ten shirts at a time to sell, so that if we clipped them, the liability would be small. The kids kept two dollars a shirt, and turned eight in to the cousins. Nothing was to stop an enterprising soul from selling ten shirts, pocketing a hundred bucks, and going home, and it occasionally happened. That, of course, would be the end of that kid's career, and the cousins were apparently not unfamiliar with violence if they managed to catch up with the scofflaw. For the most part the system worked. Word was that the cousins had spies on the street to make sure the kids didn't lie about being ripped off by our guys, but Dixie thought that was bullshit.

As the weeks and months passed, our dance in the streets with these kids became more theater than combat. It was pointless to pretend we were concertgoers; everyone knew our goddamn names. We put on a show of chasing them, and God bless them, they put on a show of running away. When we did grab somebody, we never left them dry. If a guy had six shirts, we'd take three and turn our backs while he sold the rest.

Then, just when we seemed to be settling into a decent rhythm, as always happens, management reared its ugly head.

One night, after six months on the job, our boss became obsessed with the van. I never found out why, but suddenly it was his white whale. When we met before the show that night, he announced a one-hundred-dollar bonus to each man on the team that took the van down.

We all went on the prowl, widening our usual perimeter and mostly ignoring the vendors, to their glee. After forty-five minutes, word came over the radio that someone had bagged it. They also called everyone back to our rendezvous point. There were a lot of high fives, congrats, and teasing. The two guys who found it got their bonus.

Then the boss told us that the rest of us could go home, because now that there was no contraband on the street, there would be no blowout. He explained that we wouldn't be paid for the whole shift, because we'd only worked for an hour, but he would be generous and pay us half the normal night's compensation. And hey, that's a bargain, he explained, because you're getting paid for half the night and you only worked an hour. He assured us that this was a win-win.

At the next concert, the boss made the same offer. When he left we held our own meeting. Nobody blamed the two guys who turned up the van the first time, because we did not know what the fallout would be. Now we did. Two guys get a hundred dollars, twenty guys get fucked out of half a night's pay. We didn't sugarcoat it. No one was to find the van. Everybody, including the guys who'd clipped it, was in agreement.

In practice, this sometimes required a delicate balancing act. Sometimes it required outright inventiveness. I'm not going to say that we ever directly addressed the van guys, but we did often manage to get word through Dixie or one of the other kids if their spot was getting warm. Once, when they were parked in an open-air lot near the Holland Tunnel, my partner wondered aloud to me where the van might be while he was urinating against the side of it at ten o'clock in the evening during a Madonna concert. They got out of there about five minutes before our supervisors arrived.

The night that our entire business model changed was after an Elton John concert at the Garden. It was Dixie, and I caught him with eight shirts.

"Fuck, man," he said. "This three times tonight. This shit's wrong. No way they gonna believe me."

"Who?" I asked. "The cousins?"

"Yeah, the fuckin' cousins."

I was feeling guilty. Ninety minutes earlier we'd shared an order of French fries. I took one shirt and gave him back the rest. Then I took a rolled-up order out of my back pocket and filled it out.

"Here," I said. "Show this to the cousins. They'll know it's legit. You could only get it from us."

"The fuck is this?" he asked.

"It's an order. We're supposed to serve one every time we take something. Nobody gives a fuck, but they can only come from us. The cousins will know that. I wrote down that I took eight shirts, but I'm only taking one. You can sell the other seven and keep all the bread, just give the cousins this order."

Dixie scanned the order then looked at me. "You don't gotta turn in eight shirts?"

"Shit," I said, "the other guys throw the orders in the fucking garbage. The shirts get burned. Nobody gives a fuck."

Dixie looked at me for a long minute, then, very slowly, said, "You always have these?"

I started to answer but stopped, realizing that he was trying to assess exactly how stupid I was.

"Yeah," I finally said.

He was quiet again, then nodded. "Got another one?"

I pulled the roll out of my back pocket. I probably had five or six copies. Dixie ripped the one I gave him in half.

"Make it four," he said. "Cousins be crazy I say I lost another eight. Four is good."

I initialed another order for four shirts.

Dixie smiled at me and waved the rolled-up order. "This works, we gotta talk next show."

The next show was Culture Club; it was getting cold out at night, and Dixie found me before I'd been working fifteen minutes.

"Gonna be at Mickey D's?"

"Yeah, sure."

"Let's talk," he said.

And we did.

I learned that Dixie averaged about sixty dollars a night on the shirts, and that was contingent on him selling approximately seven of every ten shirts with which he was entrusted. He skimmed a little here and there, as all the kids did, but they kept it close to the bone and the cousins didn't seem to care as long as it wasn't egregious. But, as he pointed out to me, "That magic paper changes everything."

Dixie could make sixty dollars in his first half hour of work if I gave him an order stating I took eight shirts, but only confiscated two. He could do the rest of the night legit, knowing he'd hit his mark.

"I make some coin, cousins make some coin, you get some shirts. Nobody get hurt."

Did I mention that Dixie was a lot smarter than me?

The next year was golden. We consistently got accolades

and a few bonuses for taking the most counterfeit product off the street, which we did. There were, in the beginning, a few bugs to iron out. The biggest obstacle to avoid is being a victim of your own success. It looks really bad to the supervisors if the illegally operating bootleg vendors that you're being paid to suppress are visibly seeking you out and thrusting the contraband at you. Finesse wasn't built into most of these kids, and they probably didn't rank high on patience, but Dixie schooled them and eventually everybody came around.

During high-profile shows when we knew that our supervisors were cruising around with reps from the venue, we made sure there were theatrical chases and seizures, enacting scenarios previously blocked out over Big Macs.

The kids got paid, the cousins got paid, and we collected a shitload of bogus product. I like to think Democracy was protected.

But. All good things . . .

Most of my friends worked second jobs for the same reason that mountain climbers climb mountains: because they're there. I was always more goal oriented. At my day job, when I'd go upstairs to pick up prisoners from the ninth floor in the courthouse, which was the dedicated Correction Department floor, I would look out the windows over the surrounding rooftops at a building being renovated four blocks away. It was three stories high, and had been a mattress factory. It was being developed into condominium lofts, and I was racing against the clock to accumulate a down payment on one before they hit the market. That was why, for two years, I was the private-security world's Travis Bickle. I'd work anytime, anywhere.

Then two things happened in close chronological proximity.

I hit the magic number in my savings account for the loft, and I received a promotion at work based on a test I'd taken a year earlier. Life got a lot easier, and for the first time as an adult, I didn't need two jobs to make ends meet.

So I stopped. I quit all the outside gigs and began doing fun stuff in my free time. I read. I took classes. Oh yeah, sometimes I went to concerts.

About a year after I'd given up the security work, I attended a show at the Garden. It was Dylan with Tom Petty and the Heartbreakers. I went with a childhood buddy, Vinny, who was then working as a homicide detective with the NYPD. It was a great show and we had a wonderful time. Exiting with the crowd, we were debating stopping off for a nightcap, which meant we would, and the only real question was how many and where. Then I heard a familiar voice.

"Shirts. Dylan. Ten dollars. Dylan. Dylan shirts." And there was Dixie, moving through the crowd and moving product.

I ambled up to him. "Give it to me for eight?" I said.

"Two for fifteen," he countered, turning toward me. "Oh shit!"

"Altered States?" I asked.

"Blast from the past," he responded.

He asked me if I was working shows again, and I told him that I was not. I explained that I'd actually attended this concert. The look he gave me was similar to the one I received on the night that he discovered I'd had the court orders in my pocket for six months while we'd both needlessly run through the streets.

I understood it. I'd become a civilian.

I asked how the cousins were doing.

"The cousin," he said. "Just one. Shows up with hired muscle now. Always different dudes."

"What happened to the other cousin?" I asked.

Dixie smiled and sucked his teeth.

"How's the new security?"

"Assholes," he said. "Everybody's a asshole. Nobody's happy." Then he smiled. "We had a good run though."

Two boxy guys in windbreakers popped up then, cutting through the throng toward us. One of them began yelling.

"That's unlicensed merchandise! You can't sell that here! Don't move!"

Dixie shook his head and shrugged. "Gotta go," he said, and vanished into the night. The two guys shoved past us and lumbered pointlessly after him, Rockports and Dockers fading into the crowd.

SURFING THE CRIME WAVE

On the eve of my nineteenth birthday, a group of friends took me out for a drinking tour of Lower Manhattan, the intent being to work our way south from Union Square until we arrived at the Brooklyn Bridge or passed out. There were about a dozen of us at the start of the evening, which, on a surprisingly civilized note, began with dinner at the Cedar Tavern. We stayed mostly on the East Side, veering as we moved downtown. Our second stop was a bar simply called the Pub, on Second Avenue below 14th Street. It was a fairly rough place back then, with a colorful clientele. I was shooting pool against a local when a fight broke out at the bar. After some shoving and shouting, the toothless female bartender ejected one man with the assistance of a few patrons. About fifteen minutes later, our game still in progress, a shot was fired from the street into the bar, shattering one of the small panes of glass in the windowed front door and lodging in the back wall behind us. Everyone threw themselves to the floor, and for a moment there was only the fading sound of the gunshot and the thumping bass of the Silver Convention on the jukebox. Then I heard a voice from above my hiding place half under the pool table: "Shootin' pool or what?"

I slowly stood to discover that most of the other customers were returning to their seats at the bar or scattered tables. There was some discussion about the likelihood of the shot having been fired by the gentleman recently removed. The formidable barmaid resumed pouring drinks. A couple of people stepped outside and looked around, and one or two walked to the back wall and examined the bullet hole up close.

"Pool," my opponent urged again. Though it looked as if he hadn't moved, I was fairly sure he'd hit the deck with the rest of us and was merely taking advantage of having regained his composure quicker. We finished the game and played another. I lost both and was thankful that the wager had only been one beer per game. We drank quickly and left shortly after. Emerging from the bar tentatively, as if from a foxhole, my friends and I scanned the street. There were people and cars and neon signs, and absolutely no indication that anything untoward had recently occurred. There had been no conversation in the bar about calling the police, and no cops were to be seen outside.

Several of my friends took the incident as an omen and called it a night. The rest of us kept heading south. Sometime after midnight we arrived at the Brooklyn Bridge. Four of us, myself included, lived in Brooklyn and decided to walk over the bridge to clear our heads before going home. We'd just begun our ascent up the footpath when we noticed a flurry of activity in front of One Police Plaza. There were crowds milling and lights everywhere, and we surmised they were filming a movie. We turned back off the bridge and worked our way over to the crowd.

"What's going on?" I asked someone at the periphery.

"They caught Son of Sam," he said. "Bringing him in now."

Within a few moments a disheveled-looking young man with a passing resemblance to the songwriter Don McLean was rushed past to the accompaniment of popping flashbulbs, cheers, taunts, and shouted questions. We stood there until he disappeared into the building, then resumed our hike over the bridge. On the Brooklyn side we split and went home to our separate neighborhoods. It was early morning on August 11, 1977, and, other than being my birthday, just another summer night in the city.

I find it difficult these days to explain the crime vibe of New York City back then to anyone who wasn't there. The late seventies come to me now as snapshots:

Driving home from a girlfriend's house in surreal darkness the night of the blackout, stories of looting already coming in on the car radio. The short ride made longer by every driver's trepidation at each signal-less intersection. Arriving at my corner, Eleventh Avenue, to see cars parked on the sidewalk in front of several stores, the merchants sitting on the hoods and roofs with hunting rifles and shotguns, bracing for trouble that never arrived.

Going to concerts at Fordham University, then hanging out on the roof of a friend's dormitory building, eating rice and beans and getting stoned while watching fires move across the Bronx and listening to students speculate on what was being torched. *Dry cleaner's. Pretty sure it's the dry cleaner's. Fuck no, it's the pizzeria. Shit, the pizzeria.* Much later, the subway ride home, sleeping in shifts so someone was always on guard duty.

As the seventies gave way to the eighties, as New York City teetered on the edge of bankruptcy but never fell in, most residents assumed they'd rounded some sort of historic bend and that there was light at the end of the tunnel. The eighties, of course, brought with them the advent of AIDS and the introduction of crack. We were still barreling down Dead Man's Hill, but now the brakes didn't work.

People had been freebasing cocaine for years, yet the ability to buy crack in neat little ten-dollar vials, precooked down to heart-stopping pure rock, changed the landscape of drug dealing—and street violence—in dramatic ways. The war on drugs has been and remains our generation's

Prohibition; crack was the ultimate bathtub gin. Unlike heroin, regular coke, or weed, crack transformed every street-corner dealer with a couple hundred dollars into an entrepreneur, and previously mellow junkies morphed into Wild West gunslingers. Add to the mix the federal government's shortsighted decision to take the Italian mob out of the drugs business, and it was exactly the recipe for disaster you would imagine. I suppose that if you're going to go to the trouble of having a war on drugs, it's probably a good policy to try to find out who the major players are and arrest them, but it is impossibly naive to assume that the drugs will then go away. After a series of high-profile sting operations and prosecutions like the Pizza Connection case (in which elements of the mob used pizza parlors as fronts for heroin distribution), the Italians were knocked from the top spot in the narcotics food chain. Unfortunately, the Asian gangs and Colombian cartels stepped in so quickly that, in one notoriously embarrassing incident, the FBI confessed that it had dozens of hours of wiretap tapes that could not be deciphered because none of the Chinese interpreters in the bureau were familiar with the obscure dialect of the gang under surveillance.

The way that crime affects the individual in a city like New York—if you are not being actively victimized—is in the small details of your life that change. (You feel it over time if you live here, like the aging of a spouse or a relative you see every day.) It is gradual for years, yet shocking overnight when illuminated a certain way. There are always neighborhoods you avoid, but gradually there are more. People start putting *No Radio* signs on their car windows. It begins as a hopeful deterrent to theft and vandalism, but quickly degenerates into a shameless advertisement for self-pity. The first signs that appeared were professionally printed stickers by manufacturers of security devices. *No Radio. I take it with me!* was the logo of Benzi Box, one of the first such designs. Soon, though, the signs became homemade, personalized, and increasingly desperate. *No Radio* gave way to *No radio, you already got it* and, ultimately, *Window broken three times, radio and spare gone. You got it all.* And it enraged you because you were a New Yorker, goddamn it. We didn't beg people not to steal from us. We told them they'd best not try. But there was your car, and there was your radio, and it was nighttime in Park Slope or on the Upper West Side, and you knew that green Volvo looked like an ice-cream cone to the crackhead who'd just jostled you on the sidewalk. So up went the sign and off you slunk home, spinning the cylinders on multiple high-tech locks behind you, the tumblers echoing in the empty space like the sound of cowardice.

The reaction to lawlessness in a civilized society takes many forms. There were vigilante movies like the Don Siegel–directed *Dirty Harry* (1971). Before that, Peter Boyle pulled the trigger out on hippie sex, drugs, and rock 'n' roll in the provocative counterculture exploitation flick *Joe* (1970). *Death Wish* appeared in 1974, the first film I can recall that dealt directly with New York City's escalating crime wave. It was a decade later when a guy named Bernie Goetz decided that life truly did imitate art and shot four young men who were trying to intimidate him on a subway train. I had begun my new career as a court officer in Brooklyn Criminal Court the year before, and though I considered myself a weathered New Yorker, I was overwhelmed by the steady stream of bad guys, assholes, rogues, and lost souls who filled the calendars. In my first year on the job we arraigned Joe Pepitone, the former New York Yankee accused of weapons and drug charges, and hauled Al Sharpton in numerous times on one civil-disobedience beef or another. One day I obtained Tom Waits's autograph when he arrived at the courthouse—in a somewhat impaired state—to attend the wedding of two friends who were being married by a judge in chambers.

If you were middle-aged or older in the late seventies, you probably left town or wished you could, and that was a normal response to the escalating violence. But for young people native to the city or transplanted from around the country or the planet, there is always an enticing world of possibility in disorder. Before *gentrification*, the term used in New York for people moving into rough neighborhoods was *pioneering*. And there was a definite pioneering spirit afoot. The same lawlessness that sent so much of the middle class packing was fueling a no-rules freedom in the art world, establishing a vibrant aboveground gay community, and providing fertile soil for what would emerge as the biggest movements in pop music for the next two decades, hip-hop and punk. It was a crazy, out-of-control decaying-city energy. But it was energy.

If the seventies were about chaos, the eighties and early nineties were about meanness and drugs. Creative disorder had given way to nihilism, or maybe people were just getting worn out. It was a time when drug dealers and Wall Street insider traders got fat, and the rest of us stayed home.

The changes, as I've noted, come to you in small ways. By the late eighties I'd discovered how relatively easy it was to get a parking space on the street in Manhattan. Greenwich Village, the Upper East Side, and even the Theater District—areas I'd never have dreamed of driving to—began yielding spots quickly. Racial tension, cyclically simmering and erupting here for four hundred years, flared dramatically several times. Paranoia over the fate of shrinking white enclaves led to the murders of two African American men. One, Michael Griffith, was chased to his death on a highway by a white gang in Howard Beach, Queens, in 1986; the other, Yusef Hawkins, was shot to death on a Bensonhurst street corner in 1989. Earlier that year, a young white woman jogging in Central Park was raped and beaten nearly to death.

In 1990 a group of Black activists organized the boycott of a Korean-owned fruit-and-vegetable store on Church Avenue in Brooklyn, alleging that the owners had assaulted a Black patron and falsely accused her of theft. The boycott became a blockade as protesters stood in front of the store entrance and intimidated any potential customers from shopping. A federal court issued an injunction requiring that the protesters stand at least fifty feet away from the front door. The protesters ignored it. The police ignored the protesters.

The year 1990 was also when a man in the Bronx, jealous that his girlfriend had gone out dancing, set a fire in the stairwell of the after-hours bar she'd gone to, then blocked the only exit. Eighty-seven people were killed in the Happy Land fire, and since their deaths were the result of arson, they were all characterized as murder victims, bringing the city's homicide total that year to just over 2,200. In 1991 a young Black boy was struck by a car driven by a Hasidic Jew in Crown Heights, igniting a race riot that lasted three days and resulted in the stabbing death of a rabbinical student.

I developed, suddenly, an oddly nostalgic longing for Son of Sam. Not for David Berkowitz, of course, but for a time when one man, killing six people over thirteen months, could grip New York City with fear. He was a man of his time, and lucky. If he'd struck in the early nineties, he might not have been noticed, even with his letters to the *Daily News*. After Howard Beach and Happy Land, the Central Park jogger and the Crown Heights riot, a plain old serial killer seemed kind of quaint to me. Middle American, like a town that still had a milkman or a doctor who made house calls.

By 1993 the sinking-ship pathos was unavoidable, and New Yorkers had had their fill. Ed Koch, mayor for three terms, had vowed to become New York City's first four-term mayor, but in 1989 he was unable to secure the nomination of the Democratic Party, which went instead to David Dinkins, the Manhattan borough president. Dinkins was challenged by a Republican upstart named Rudy Giuliani. Rudy had made his bones as a federal prosecutor and had a reputation as a take-no-prisoners tough guy. New York was almost ready for him, but not quite. In one of the tightest elections in city history, Dinkins defeated Giuliani and became New York's first African American mayor.

The crime wave continued unabated, and if people had become frustrated by Koch's hands-in-the-air attitude toward anarchy, they despised Dinkins's fatherly social-worker stance. *There's no such thing as a bad boy*, his demeanor conveyed, often at a crime scene where grisly evidence was being carted away behind him. In the summer of 1992 there was a surge in sexual assaults committed against young girls at public swimming pools. Gangs of boys would surround them in the water, trap them in a circle, and grope them. The street term for this type of assault was *whirlpool*. As the number of incidents increased and media coverage became intense, Mayor Dinkins called a press conference.

He unveiled a plan to appeal directly to the decency of the young men of New York City's streets. He displayed several advertising buttons with slogans. The two most memorable were *Don't Dis Your Sis* and *Whirlpool Ain't Cool*. Dinkins beamed for the cameras. I have always believed that moment cost him the next election. In 1993 Rudy Giuliani won the race by the same slender margin by which he'd previously lost.

The first time I'd seen Giuliani on television was at a press conference years earlier, with then senator Alfonse D'Amato. They had donned biker outfits, gone up to Washington Heights, and bought crack. Their intent, apparently, was to show that anyone at all could obtain drugs in the neighborhood, and to that end they were certainly successful. They looked like refugees from the Greenwich Village Halloween Parade. If someone sold them drugs, I thought, maybe we really did have a problem.

I confess to being among the early Giuliani supporters when he was first elected. We'd had enough, and it was time to fight back. Rudy's quality-of-life initiatives seemed silly, but cleaning graffiti, fixing broken windows, and getting rid of squeegee guys actually did create an impression that crime—or street crimes, at any rate—were no longer encouraged through municipal neglect.

The new administration was not without its critics. There were many complaints from the African American community about the random stopping and frisking of young men. The gay community was displeased with the crackdown on clubs and bathhouses, and in both Chinatown and largely Italian American neighborhoods like Bensonhurst, no one was happy with the zero-tolerance policy on fireworks.

As uneasy as many New Yorkers were with Giuliani's aggressive policies, the crime rate did plunge. Murder statistics quickly dropped to their lowest point in twenty, then thirty years. In 1997 Rudy was reelected with such an encouraging mandate that he expanded his platform. The war on crime had been transformed—at least for Giuliani—into a referendum on civilized society, and he was determined to mold one.

After crime, the next publicly identified threat to social welfare was commercial sex, at least at street level. Giuliani waged a successful war on pornography and topless bars—any establishment that sold pornographic material was required to devote two-thirds of its space to nonpornographic interests, and topless bars had to be located more than five hundred feet from any residential housing. Many strip joints, especially in Manhattan, folded. The adult bookstores and video shops that could hold on complied— five thousand dusty copies of *The Sound of Music* and old crossword-puzzle magazines up front, the backs crowded with magazines, videos, sex toys, and lube.

The city thus safeguarded, attention turned to other important topics: jaywalking and motorists not properly seat-belted. Fences were erected at a number of Midtown intersections, those impudent enough to bound or walk around them threatened with arrest. Likewise, in a town where it is impossible to achieve speeds exceeding twelve miles per hour, priority was now placed on making sure that everyone was wearing their harness. Checkpoints were set up at random corners. I was stopped and pulled over by a foot patrolman while waiting at a red light. (Fortunately, I was in compliance.)

There comes a moment in the movie *Bananas* when Woody Allen, having aided in a fictional South American country's revolution, stands proudly next to the rebel leader as he outlines the new government policy. Woody smiles and nods at each initiative until the leader states that every citizen must wear clean underwear, and that underwear will be worn on the outside to facilitate inspections. Woody's expression in that scene was a lot like mine as I drove away from my random seat-belt stop in my new squeaky-clean, porn-free, trigger-happy cop town. I was not alone. That expression marked the visages of many New Yorkers—a look that asked, *What next?*

Then came September 11, 2001. It is not my intent to dwell on the events of that day in political or even historical context. It was, however, the most devastating crime ever committed against the city of New York, and should be mentioned as such. Two close friends of mine lost their sons, and many other friends and acquaintances were similarly devastated. I was in my car, stopped at a red light, about fifteen blocks north of the World Trade Center, when the second plane hit. I saw it happen. I saw a huge chunk of the building tear away and fall. I ran the light and headed east for the bridge to Brooklyn, steering around slower-moving vehicles and not braking for any traffic signals until I was safely over the bridge. I was wearing my seat belt.

Since 9/11, crime seems to be defined differently. Every reference to the pre-9/11 world—as bad as it may have been—seems hopelessly sugarcoated. There was a short period of time—weeks, really—when rules just didn't matter. I returned home from work three days after the attack to find a fire engine parked awkwardly, half on the sidewalk, in front of my neighborhood bar. I entered to find a dozen or so firefighters, still in full gear, covered in ash, drinking silently. They had not been off duty in thirty-six hours, and had lost an untold number of comrades. The entire city comported itself in a similarly shell-shocked manner for longer than any of us can realistically recall, until, bit by bit, there was a return. To parking tickets and burglaries. To littering and muggings. To graffiti and drug dealing. To normal crime.

Never have a people so welcomed it.

OPENING DAY

The weather was perfect on June 21, 2005, as I rode the N train to KeySpan Park for the fifth opening-day home game of the Brooklyn Cyclones. I am one of those New Yorkers who chronically laments the Disneyfication of the city—particularly Times Square and Coney Island—but hasn't missed an opening day yet. I like to think of myself as part of the problem.

The renovation of the Coney Island station was finally complete, and you could ride directly to the shore once again. It's an odd, retro-modern-looking stop now, like something out of *The Jetsons*, or the old TWA terminal at JFK. Forty years ago it would have been the coolest space imaginable. Now it looks instantly archaic, like modern Soviet architecture. There's nothing worse than old cool. Plus, they destroyed all the shops that had inhabited the station. The Terminal Bar and Philip's Candy were my favorites. The bar had been closed for years, but the candy shop remained open for business up until the station began its renovation. It had been there since 1907, and I remember the day that my friend Andy discovered his grandfather in a photograph of customers, taped to the store window, that was dated 1930.

I had set off for the game directly from my job, so I'd taken the R at Borough Hall and switched to the N at DeKalb Avenue. I was on the express for about twenty seconds when the announcement sounded over the public-address system: *"Passenger Timmy McLoughlin, please report to the motorman's booth."*

It was Kenny Garguilo. We had first met more than twenty years earlier when we both worked in the textbook department at the main branch of Barnes & Noble; and being a couple of white ethnic outer-borough kids with little regard for higher education and no predilection for crime, we chased each other through the civil-service system for a couple of decades. Kenny had been a 911 operator, then a cop, before becoming a motorman. I was a night watchman for the Transit Authority before becoming a court officer, then a court clerk. I run into Kenny once or twice a year, either on the subway or at Nathan's in Coney Island during his meal break.

I looked for the motorman's booth—as instructed— receiving questioning glances from fellow straphangers as I made my way through the cars. I could see people wondering if I was really important or just a terrorist. Kenny and I caught up on old times and traded war stories for a while, then I left him alone to chauffeur me the rest of the way to the stadium.

Talking to Kenny brought my Transit Authority days back in a rush. I've always had the love-hate relationship with the system that one feels for the company in a company town. My father and two uncles were career transit workers. Uncle Mike was a bus driver, and Uncle Charlie was a mechanic, working on subway motors and undercarriages. My father was a boiler maintainer, heating the enormous repair shops called "carbarns" in Coney Island, East New York, and 207th Street in Manhattan.

My own very brief career was, as I said, that of a night watchman. Of course, since garbage collectors are sanitation engineers, and meter maids are traffic-enforcement agents, my title could not officially be "night watchman." I was a property-protection agent. Really. On my first day I was issued a blue hat that looked vaguely police-ish and a little yellow plastic flashlight, and I was assigned the midnight-to-eight shift in the Coney Island yards, there to ensure, in the mid-1980s, that no one would place any graffiti on the thousand or so subway cars housed in my area of the seventy-five-acre yard. In a very small way, I understood the frustration of a Border Patrol officer with two hundred miles to monitor and nine hours of darkness to contend with. It was a job defined by acceptable levels of failure.

Every night I would relieve the four-to-twelve man, sign in, and begin my clock winds, which involved carrying a large, heavy, ancient clock, sheathed in leather and outfitted with a shoulder strap, around the train yard once every hour. At five or six locations along the fence line, there were small metal containers, about the size of ashtrays in a car. Each container held a key secured by a chain. The key was to be inserted into a slot in the back of the clock and turned, causing an indentation in the tape that spooled its way through the innards of the gizmo, thus recording that you were where you were supposed to be, when you were supposed to be there. Sturdy as the clocks were, most of the watchmen figured out how to disable them pretty quickly, and often spent the night sitting in the little phone booth–like shacks on the periphery of the yards. In East New York you learned to unscrew the lightbulb so no one shot at you. In the morning the trains were covered in graffiti, you filled out a report, and then you went home. It was a full life.

On the rare occasion when I did encounter a graffiti artist—or vandal, as my profession mandated I regard them—I would chase them away rather than detain them. With absolutely no training, no police or peace officer status, and only the aforementioned yellow flashlight for equipment, I did not exactly see my job in a law enforcement context. I felt more like the ranger in Jellystone Park, ever vigilant to prevent Yogi Bear from snatching picnic baskets. I think the graffiti kids felt the same way. They always gave me the courtesy of running away when I confronted them, even if they were in a group. I came to recognize some of the regulars, and they would casually acknowledge me outside the train yard if I walked over to Spumoni Gardens for my meal break. I generally considered them harmless, but was once rocked from my idyll when they torched a stolen car across the street from the yard, about thirty feet from my booth. It was two thirty in the morning, and I'd been on the phone with a friend who worked the night shift in a brokerage house on Wall Street. I was sitting with my back to the street, and first saw the flames reflected in the glass of the booth. That resulted in the one and only 911 call of my career.

If I did not get to know the muralists up close, I certainly studied my coworkers intensely. They were in many ways more tribal than the graffiti kids. Every train yard has its own ethnic vibe, and Coney Island's was distinctly Italian. Small but elaborate gardens were planted anywhere there was a bare patch of earth, and rows of tomato plants were staked between the tracks. The number of running trains is cut down dramatically at night, yet since the system never shuts down, repair and maintenance work goes on 24/7.

I worked in several yards by the end of that summer. As the new man, I was assigned vacation relief, which meant that I moved around the city, filling in a week here and there as people took time off. I'd cut through the barns on my winds, or on breaks, and watch the work crews—called gangs—roam the floor, then pounce on a subway car as though it were a wounded critter cut from the herd. Six to eight men would jump into the pit below the car and yank more machinery from the undercarriage than would be expected on a space shuttle. In three or four hours it was all replaced, and they would move to another car and begin again.

During the day each yard was as bustling and self-contained as a small town, but even at night there was a good level of activity. I'd grown up in and around the yards, and what strikes me as unusual about them now is that, back then, they did not strike me as an unusual place at all.

The barns are huge and built like airplane hangars. There might be more than a thousand men working at peak hours. Just men, by the way. During my stint, the train yards, carbarns, and machine shops were an entirely masculine domain. The whole compound resembled an army base as much as a village.

Although my job was generally considered to be preventing theft or damage to property from outside sources, we were also supposed to watch for infractions of rules by employees. Since one of the rules was that no unauthorized persons were permitted in the yards, and since I'd spent the night sleeping on a cot in the boiler room of most of those yards in the summertime when I was a kid, I kind of took that rule as more of a suggestion.

When I worked there, anything and everything was for sale. In Coney Island I could buy condoms or prayer cards from various entrepreneurs operating out of their lockers. At 207th Street there was a corner of the barn known as Mulberry Street, where, on Fridays, all the clothing and merchandise was displayed.

At the 39th Street yard, which was relatively small and always smelled of diesel fuel because it housed work trains, the signal maintainers kept dogs. There were five of them, and on the few occasions I was sent there, they patiently waited for me outside my booth and walked with me as I made my winds.

A dozen or more of the men lived in each yard, their numbers shifting as people got divorced, got evicted, or just became crazy. The ones who became crazy stayed the longest, and I remember one who cried when his foreman told him he had to leave because he'd retired.

There were odd, makeshift living spaces rigged in closets and small rooms. At 207th Street I saw two men living in the motor room above the freight elevator, sleeping on rollaway beds on opposite sides of the enormous, loud engine. They bathed in homemade showers, did laundry in concrete garage sinks, and dried their clothing by draping it over subway cars they were repairing. Though no one had shown me a written rule stating that employees were not to reside at their work site, I was pretty sure this was not what the city government had in mind.

Workers cooked on the many stoves and refrigerators in the barns—also prohibited—and at the two full kitchens cobbled together in Coney Island, and the three in upper Manhattan. To their credit, the guys at 207th Street painted the fridges to blend with the walls, or hid them in the rear of the workshops. Some men prepared elaborate breakfasts and lunches and sold them to coworkers, operating little side businesses. I felt rather like Claude Rains in *Casablanca* when, years after my departure, I read that a surprise inspection had revealed over one hundred refrigerators and stoves at the upper Manhattan barn. A photo showed them piled in a heap in the parking lot. I was shocked, shocked, to discover the contraband had been on the premises.

What was most surprising about all of the eccentricity I encountered was its one solid tie to unwavering logic. From the pack rats of Coney Island, filling entire storage rooms with their scavenged treasures, to the mountain men of 207th Street, carrying hunting bows across Broadway to unload quivers into paper targets propped against mountains of salt in the unmanned Sanitation Department warehouse, everyone adhered to the golden rule. Their term for it was "making service," and it was remarkably simple: the trains had to run. Whatever else happened, you had to make service. And they did. I think all of them—from the conscientious to the shiftless to the just plain nuts—understood that the reason their fringe society could exist as it did in the middle of New York City was that things ran smoothly. When things do not run smoothly, management sticks in its ugly proboscis. And as any blue-collar worker can attest, management's idea of solving a problem is throwing all your refrigerators away and declaring the problem solved, usually without knowing what the problem is.

So the trains ran, and continue to run, I noted, as we slowed to a lazy stop in the newly renovated Coney Island station. As part of the Transit Authority's recent efforts to distract public attention from mounting fare increases and its own very private books, it ballyhooed advances in modernization, cost cutting, and public service. Don't believe the hype. The trains always ran, and the trains will always run, largely because of strange guys with wrenches and welding torches and grinding wheels. Guys who brainstorm tools to fix problems unforeseen by manufacturers, who then create those tools on the spot in the blacksmith shop. Guys whose bosses will keep throwing out refrigerators to show *their* bosses that they can solve problems. And their bosses will keep trying to flense the workplace of fun and eccentricity until it is as sanitized and bland as the new Coney Island station. And they'll fail. At least they have, I'm pleased to say, for the past two generations.

By the way, the Cyclones won that night 10–7. Fifth straight opening-day win, and against the hated Staten Island Yankees no less. There's nothing like enjoying a hot dog and a cold beer while watching a ball game and a Coney Island sunset. Of course there's also Neil Diamond's video image exhorting you to join him in singing "Sweet Caroline" during the seventh-inning stretch, and way too many chintzy advertising plugs, but, as I've established, I'm part of the problem.

I dozed briefly on the N during the ride home, and awakened startled and momentarily disoriented. I checked my feet instinctively, always remembering my father's admonition that if you fell asleep on the subway someone would steal your shoes. But I was having a good day. They were still there.

MAHARAJA FOR A YEAR (1999–2000)

I am old. Officially middle-aged. I've got a receding hair-line, an impressive beer gut, and failing vision that threatens bifocals in the near future. I wear Dockers and Van Heusen shirts to my anonymous civil-service job, and I worry about how late Springsteen is going to play next Wednesday, because, after all, I have to get up early the next morning. I'm your average slob. A mere mortal, like you. You wouldn't notice me on the subway at rush hour, or on line in the supermarket. But once, a long time ago, I was a maharaja.

I awakened one day to find myself forty, single again, and at loose ends. My uncle Charley, having recently retired, had developed a fondness for Atlantic City, and I began to accompany him on his one-weekend-a-month jaunts. It was fun getting out of town, driving down to South Jersey, and leaving the real world behind for a few days. Neither of us had ever been gamblers, so we just bummed around, playing twenty-five-cent slot machines and wandering on the boardwalk. At first we stayed in cheap motels off the strip, but after a few visits we began to get discounted rooms from the casinos, and that made them cheaper options than the fleabags, so we availed ourselves. What amazed me from the first were the inducements offered at our paltry level of play.

Of course, over time, the quarter slots became boring, and we moved up to fifty-cent and dollar machines. Eventually the table games called, and we watched the action, trying to figure them out, trying to work up the nerve to sit down at one. My uncle purchased gaming software, and we learned the most basic rules of blackjack, which required some small level of skill, and roulette, which was nothing but a game of luck. I played many games on the computer, and discovered that, although in the long term I could never win at anything, I could certainly lose slowly at blackjack, and occasionally have a grand winning moment at roulette. After hundreds of virtual games, we were almost ready for some real green-felt action. But where?

During our visits, my uncle and I had stayed at the Showboat, Harrah's, and Caesars, among others, and had toured all of the casinos, playing at least a little while in most. But nothing, in our experience, rivaled the Taj Mahal. It was as if Donald Trump, New York City's prince of garish excess, had indulged a drug-fueled fantasy of chrome, smoked mirrors, plush carpeting, and big bathtubs. How could you not love this place? If you're going to abandon good taste and good sense at the same time, why do it halfway? The Taj Mahal was the iconic casino to us, and it was there we would take the plunge.

We checked in and settled down for lunch. After a dozen or so trips, our discounted rooms had become free rooms, as long as we stayed only one night, Monday through Thursday. Not bad if you're retired, but I was burning precious vacation days. After a brainstorming session over cheeseburgers and beer, we decided to start with roulette. A no-skill game seemed just right for two guys with no skills. We pooled our agreed-upon bankroll, a hundred dollars each, and headed out. It had been decided that I would place the bets for both of us, on this, our first venture into what we hoped would be a new major vice in our lives.

I probably needn't point out the special kind of mental illness required to devise "strategies" for playing a game where you watch a ball roll around for a while and then stop somewhere, but otherwise reasonable people have come up with them anyway.

There's the biased-wheel theory, which postulates that after many thousands of spins, even the most meticulously maintained wheel will acquire microscopic wear and grooves, causing the ball to favor certain numbers. My uncle and I called this "chasing doubles," because we were often drawn to tables where the same number had repeated at least once in very few spins. Another theory has it that you wait for a color, black or red, to come out three times in a row, then bet the other way. This theory also requires doubling your bet every time you lose, until you win. Of course, if you could do that, you wouldn't be sitting at a five-dollar-minimum roulette table—you would be in the roped-off, high-roller area with the rest of the people who can afford a serious gambling problem.

As we approached the table, my uncle reassured me. "Don't be nervous," he said. "It's only two hundred bucks. We could lose it anyway on a bad night with the machines. Just pick one strategy and stick with it. And be conservative, no more than fifteen a spin. I'll keep track if you start winning, and I'll tell you when we should go."

"Okay," I said. "Fifteen sounds good." At fifteen dollars a spin I could cover three numbers, or bet ten on the almost-even-money plays, like colors, or even and odd, and still have five for a long shot.

We'd figured that on a busy table the wheel was spun about thirty times per hour. If I had a total losing streak, I'd still be able to play for about twenty minutes, and if I could hit every so often on even money, who knew?

It was a relatively quiet night, but at the Taj that meant

a low roar. I took a seat at the far end of the table from the wheel. There were four other players; a young Asian croupier worked the game. I waited until the spin was completed, and placed two one-hundred-dollar bills on the felt as she raked in the losing bets.

"Singles?" she asked. Everyone else had been betting large quantities of one-dollar chips, seeming to place them everywhere on the table except on the number which had come out, twelve.

"No," I said, then paused and lowered my voice. "Nickels." That was casino jargon for a five-dollar chip. I was very proud of myself. She looked at me like I was a sixty-five-year-old hippie who'd just said that something was groovy, and wordlessly slid me a stack of chips.

Everything that occurred after that happened very quickly. I'd decided to go with the biased-wheel theory, chasing doubles, because I'm stupider than most people. Twelve was a black number and I put ten dollars on black, so as not to bet against myself, and five on number twelve. It was only fifteen dollars, but, honestly, my hand shook a little. It wasn't the money, though the idea of losing fifteen dollars every four minutes was a little disconcerting. It was the atmosphere. Little old ladies played the slots. I was at a table game, with tough guys and molls. Of course everyone else who was playing that night looked like they sold aluminum siding.

My uncle stood behind my chair silently as the croupier released the ball. Double zero. We lost. Everyone did. I placed five dollars on double zero, five dollars on twelve, and five dollars on black. The croupier released the ball again, and twelve came out. I won. This was when my uncle began speaking in tongues, apparently possessed by the spirit of Legs Diamond.

"Play twelve again," he said, whispering loudly and speaking fast. "Fifty dollars. And put fifty on black. Play double zero again. Come on. Play even. Double your bets."

"What happened to no more than fifteen dollars a spin, and stick with one strategy?" I asked, looking at him over my shoulder.

"My palm is itchy." He showed it to me. "It means we're lucky."

"Oh."

I repeated the same pattern of twelve, double zero, and black, my only concession to my uncle's sudden lunacy being that I placed ten dollars on black. Double zero came in, and I'd won again. I sat there for another fifteen minutes or so, winning and losing. Mostly losing, I think, but the wins, when they came, were impressive. I found that I couldn't keep track of anything, and began to feel foolish. And my uncle, who had sworn that the betting decisions would be my call, was still demanding that I place enormous sums of money on numbers that randomly occurred to him, some of which were not represented on the wheel. I stood quickly and gathered my chips, gave the croupier a five-dollar chip as I'd seen other people do, and left the table.

My uncle and I argued about leaving in the middle of my "hot streak" as we walked to the cashier's window. We cashed out at $565, and burst into stunned laughter.

"How do they stay in business?" my uncle joked.

We used our winnings that day to up our stake to two hundred dollars each for future trips, and that's pretty much where it stayed. Some trips we won, some we went home broke, most of the time we lost a little and had to replenish our supply for the following trip.

Two or three visits after we had begun playing the tables, we each received a letter inviting us to make use of something called the Bengal Club, a free bar and buffet room just off the casino floor. It was, we were soon to learn, the entry level of three "clubs" that the Taj Mahal provided as perks for regular players. The next was the President's Club, also off the casino floor. This was a slightly more formal room, with waiters and tablecloths, but essentially the same food as the Bengal Club. Finally, there was the Maharaja Club, on the fiftieth floor, with spectacular views, elegant meals, an impressive bar, and a piano lounge. The Maharaja Club required a special key for the elevator and a photo on your gaming card. We began to study our fellow players, and tried to rank their stature in terms of the clubs.

A month after getting the letter inviting us to be Bengals, I received another, telling me I was now in the President's Club. My uncle Charley received no such letter. When our monthly "offers" arrived, they also differed for the first time. His was the same as always: a free room any Monday through Thursday, discounts here and there, and a few five-dollar vouchers for the tables. My package stated that I was entitled to a free room any night of the week, and free tickets to see Natalie Cole, who would be performing there soon.

Bear in mind, on our first venture to table play, I did the gambling. On the next trip, Uncle Charley did. After that, we always sat together at slow, low-action tables, playing roulette, blackjack, or a silly game called Let It Ride. My point is, my uncle having settled down emotionally before his first betting session, we'd both maintained our comfortable nickel-and-dime wagering patterns. And we always played together. Give or take a few bucks, we were betting exactly the same amount of money. This was true even when we played the slots. We usually sat side by side and bullshitted over coffee or cocktails while we fed the machines.

These trips were more social occasions than anything really connected to gambling. Any important news or big discussion was intentionally put on hold until the monthly two-and-a-half-hour run. In fact, "we have to take a ride to AC" became our code for a serious talk, or major philosophical debate.

The following month I received a letter informing me that I was now a member of the Maharaja Club, and instructing me to have my photo taken for my new Taj card. When my monthly offers arrived, they included a free *suite* any night of the week, free tickets to see Ringo Starr, and, if I arrived on the specified night, a free thirteen-inch color television. I called my uncle, who informed me that his package had not changed.

Over the next year we made about fifteen trips to Atlantic City, during which I'd always stay in a suite. I did in fact pick up the color TV, and on subsequent visits a VCR, a bookshelf stereo system, a Dirt Devil vacuum cleaner, and a nice set of Henckels chef's knives. I went to nightclub shows, many that I would normally not be caught dead at, and passionately debated their relative merit with my uncle. These included the aforementioned Ringo and Natalie Cole (Natalie twice, second time worlds better—not even close), Shirley Bassey, Tom Jones, and the Righteous Brothers. I obtained my key and photo ID, and we dined in the Maharaja Club, listening to quiet jazz, enjoying football on the giant TV in the afternoons, and sipping mimosas with brunch in the mornings.

We never reconciled why I had been chosen for such preferential treatment when my uncle's gambling pattern was virtually identical, but then, it never really bothered either one of us. The Maharaja Club was good for two; I always got two tickets to any event, and the toys were just that, frivolous giveaways. My uncle conjectured that perhaps I was logging in more table play than he, since occasionally I'd remain for an hour or so after he went up to sleep. I didn't know. We'd figured that all perks were based on playing time and not winning or losing. Casinos know that if you stay long enough, you *will* lose. But even if I lost my stake every trip, I didn't see how this worked out for them.

I constructed a convoluted scenario in which, if you monitored my wagering pattern over a given weekend, I was betting three or four thousand dollars, albeit ten bucks or so at a time. What difference did it make if I never won or lost much more than eighty dollars? I was showing them *action*, goddamnit, and that was what got you the perks.

Here's the truly disturbing bit: *I began to believe this.*

Having convinced myself that I was earning these freebies by moving two hundred dollars around the tables one weekend a month, I began to act like a maharaja. So did my uncle. When I called to reserve our suite, I always did so through a casino host, not the normal reservation number provided with my offers. I would request that my uncle's free room be granted us for a Friday or Saturday, and that it adjoin my suite. By doing so we were able to create two-bedroom, three-bathroom apartments. I always requested rooms on a high floor with an ocean view. When we arrived, if the accommodations were not satisfactory I would again contact a casino host, who was usually able to relocate us.

This reached a crescendo the weekend that my girlfriend decided to join us. She watched as I rejected our first suite, then, after I'd accepted the next, my uncle called down to complain about a lightbulb being out in the closet of his adjoining room. While we waited for someone to replace the bulb, I again contacted my casino host and requested a room-service comp, saying we were too tired to go up to the club.

"Why are you acting this way?" my girlfriend asked. "You're not like this."

I wanted to explain that I was a maharaja, but I knew she wouldn't understand.

A few weeks later she mentioned that a country music singer she liked was performing at the Taj Mahal, and that she'd love to see the show. "No problem," I said, seeing this as an opportunity to flex my muscles and score points at the same time. I picked up the phone and called the casino. I told the host who I was and that I wanted a suite for the following weekend—high floor, ocean view, of course. Two tickets to the show, and some meal comps for the room, if it wasn't too much trouble. I sat on hold for a few minutes, and then a rather formal voice I didn't recognize, a woman's, came on the line.

"I'm sorry, Mr. McLoughlin, you're not qualified for tickets to that show, or for a complimentary suite."

"What?" I said. Always a master of the snappy comeback.

"I'm sorry. You're not cleared for these comps."

I asked—being pointlessly arrogant—to whom I was speaking. When the woman identified herself, I requested that she check my status again. While on hold, I smiled at my girlfriend, watching me from across the room. I tried to affect a look of patient endurance, but there was an unpleasant tingling beginning at the back of my neck.

"Mr. McLoughlin?" the host returned. "I'm sorry to keep you waiting. We review the wagering patterns of customers periodically. Slot players are reviewed quarterly, table players annually. Your offers have been based on the level of play exhibited on your first visit. Unfortunately, you've never again matched that level."

"That's not true," I said honestly. "I've wagered about the same on every trip for over a year."

"No, sir. We show that on your first visit you wagered an average of fifteen hundred dollars per spin on roulette. You've never repeated that."

"How much?"

"Fifteen hundred dollars a spin, for just over an hour. I can see if we have a room and tickets, if you'd care to purchase them. Sir?"

Webster's New World Dictionary defines *mahout* as "the

keeper or driver of elephants." Basically, the guy who walks behind them with a shovel. It's a long drop from maharaja to mahout. I spiraled smoothly down the hole as I realized that everything I had enjoyed and deluded myself into believing I'd earned for the past year had been based on a misplaced decimal point on a pit boss's clipboard.

It ended just that quickly. My girlfriend never did get to see the country music show. We're married now, and very happy. My uncle still goes to Atlantic City occasionally. He sometimes stays at the Taj Mahal, though I think he's begun favoring Harrah's, and a newer place, the Borgata. I hardly ever make the trips anymore. I took the ride with him some time ago, after not having visited for a couple of years. It was all right, but certainly not the same. We waited on line to check in, then paid for dinner.

Talking to other guests, I discovered that they had temporarily closed the Maharaja Club, and its members had to use the President's Club until it reopened. I extended my sympathies to those affected and agreed with them that this was no way to retain your A-list players. Then I sat at a hot twenty-five-cent Elvis Presley slot and quickly turned my ten-dollar stake into seventeen dollars and fifty cents.

"How do they stay in business?" I asked my uncle as we strolled out onto the boardwalk, two mahouts on the prowl.

ABRAHAM, MARTIN, AND GREG SCARPA

As I write this, today is Martin Luther King Jr.'s birthday, and as happens every year on the anniversary of his birth, my thoughts turn to Brooklyn mob boss Greg Scarpa. How could they not? I picture streets across America's inner-city neighborhoods being renamed Greg Scarpa Boulevard, or maybe a statue in a park in Laurel, Mississippi, that darling little town that is presently featured on an HGTV series.

Perhaps a bronze bust of the crazed one-eyed gangster is what's needed to remind residents of their town's less-than-quaint racial past.

Perhaps not.

But for me, Scarpa will always be inextricably linked to the civil rights movement, and serves as an example of the numerous deals with devils we've made as we lurched through the past century and a half, trying to make this country work for everyone in it—the people we stole it from, those we brought over in chains to build it, and we the thieves. Quite a balancing act, and always a day for reflection. And what better place for quiet reflection than a church?

I remember my first cup of coffee like I remember my first kiss. I had just finished serving mass at Saint Rosalia up on Fourteenth Avenue. It was the six thirty a.m. weekday mass, celebrated in Italian. For a brief time, maybe four months or so, I was the youngest altar boy in the history of the parish, and this was during that time. I'd walked the seven blocks from my apartment in predawn darkness, and even after the service it was late enough in the year that I stepped out of the church tentatively, like some crepuscular animal, onto 63rd Street. But the deli on the opposite corner was open, so what the hell. I walked in and, probably for the first time, affected that distracted, disinterested look I would trot out in the next decade to try to gain entrance to bars and porn theaters, to ask out girls who were clearly not in my league, to obtain jobs for which I was woefully unqualified. Though these attempts mostly failed, there would be moments when I was golden. This was that kind of morning. The bald middle-aged man behind the counter barely registered my presence, which was all I could hope for. One minute and ten cents later I was walking home with a steaming cup of coffee, regular, whatever that meant. I slung my cassock and surplice over my shoulder like Frank Sinatra with his tuxedo jacket, took a tentative sip, and strolled home as the sun rose. This, I was certain, was a defining moment. Cut me a little slack, I was eight years old.

I liked serving funeral masses, because most of them were during the week, which required being excused from school. By third grade it had become clear to me that my relationship with academia would be contentious and, I hoped, as short-lived as New York State law would allow. I wisely kept it to myself, but I felt caged in class, almost always bored, and keenly aware that whatever I could see outside the classroom window was more exciting than anything going on inside. Plus, our teachers were nuns. Let's just say they were rarely kind.

I was serving what I believe was my second funeral mass, with an older altar boy named Frank, when I received my first tip. All of the other altar boys were older than I was, but Frank was a real upperclassman, probably a seventh grader. A man in a suit from the funeral home called us over after the service. He thanked us, out on the steps of the church, and shook our hands. He palmed me something, and I looked down to see that it was money. Frank's disappeared into his pocket in a quick, practiced motion, which I clumsily tried to imitate. When the man left, I asked Frank what was up.

"It's a tip," he said. "You get them at weddings all the time, funerals are like fifty-fifty. Father Sforza says we have to give him half. Says it's for the altar boys fund."

"There's an altar boys fund?" I asked.

"If there is I haven't seen it. Just keep your fucking mouth shut."

So I went home that day with three dollars in my pocket. My weekly allowance had recently been raised from fifty cents to seventy cents—"A dime a day," my father had proudly declared. I kept my fucking mouth shut and added my name to the sign-up sheet for weddings, which I'd previously ducked because they were almost always on weekends, and I hadn't seen an upside to being in church on my own time.

Wedding tips averaged five dollars per altar boy, sometimes a staggering ten. I served at masses for five years, third grade through eighth, and I'm pleased to say that in all that time I only got bagged by Father Sforza twice, and had to forfeit half my bounty.

Vincent Sforza was the priest in charge of the altar boys at Regina Pacis when I was in third grade. Back then, boys were allowed to volunteer to serve mass only beginning in the fourth. I approached the priest one day after school and said I was ready to be an altar boy. He told me that third graders weren't mature enough to learn the duties. I replied that maybe the others weren't, but I was. He laughed, and agreed to let me try. I served for the rest of that term. Beginning the following year, third graders were allowed to sign up.

Learning the ropes was pretty simple. There were six or seven times you had to ring bells or deliver water and wine, and most important, follow the priest around with a small gold plate on a stick, keeping it under the chalice to catch any bits of Jesus that might drop while he administered Communion. Once you learned the routine, everything was done by rote. That left a lot of time for daydreaming, my favorite pastime then as now.

I spent most of my time looking up, though not heavenward. There was a large, impressive mural that spanned the church ceiling. At the top was the Trinity, Jesus and God the Father with arms extended, resting on comfy clouds, holding a golden crown between them. Above them hovered the Holy Spirit in the form of a dove, casting a ray of light onto the crown. Directly beneath sat Mary, flanked and trailed by a descending pantheon of angels and saints. Finally, at the foot of the piece, were the worshippers looking adoringly toward the deity. Among those I recognized on the ground were Monsignor Cioffe, our pastor, and a man reputed to be mob boss Joseph Profaci.

It was common knowledge in the neighborhood that Profaci, along with the monsignor, had organized fundraising for the church and donated quite a sum himself. And even as children, though it had taken place before we were born, we all knew the story of the diamonds.

* * *

The parish in which I lived was technically Saint Rosalia, and that was the name of the old church on Fourteenth Avenue where I lost my coffee virginity. That structure dated to the 1890s. Even in my day, it was past its prime, but it had a small, worn-down beauty. Our parish had two churches, the other being Regina Pacis. Regina was huge compared to Saint Rosalia, and modernish, though gaudy. It was constructed just after World War II with funds raised entirely by the largely immigrant Italian community that sat at the juncture of Bay Ridge, Bensonhurst, and Borough Park. The church and its attendant buildings, school, convent, rectory, and such occupied almost a full city block.

The church opened its doors in 1951. If I haven't been clear about this, no expense was spared. Two thousand tons of Italian marble had been imported, exquisite wood, the aforementioned ceiling mural painted by an Italian artist brought in for the commission. But, at the end of the day, the crowning jewel of the church was its crown jewels. Rising behind the altar was a large portrait of the Madonna and child. This is, after all, *Regina Pacis*, and Mary is the "Queen of Peace." She and the infant Jesus are depicted with crowned halos. Between those hardworking immigrants and the dubitable mob money, Mary and the infant's crowns were eighteen-carat gold, encrusted with over six hundred diamonds.

The basilica was dedicated with a high mass in the summer of 1951. In January 1952, Father Cioffi flew to Rome with the jewels and had both crowns blessed by Pope Pius XII. Eight days after he returned and mounted them over the altar, they were stolen.

There is enough neighborhood legend surrounding that theft to fill a book, but there are also verifiable facts. One week after they were stolen, the jewels were returned, anonymously, in a special-delivery postal envelope mailed to the rectory. Newspapers across the city hailed it as a miracle. The *New York Journal-American* was indicative of that reporting:

> *The theft and return of the two jewel-studded crowns is one of those rare stories that touch the heart with wonder and affirm the intimation we all have of power beyond our little reason. Prayer goes beyond our reason and works in a way we do not understand. We think the Pastor of Regina Pacis Votive Shrine spoke the absolute truth when he said those prayers had been answered.*

I'm sure most of the neighborhood residents believed that it had been their faith and prayers that resulted in the return of the gems, just as I'm sure they thought it a mere coincidence that twenty-two-year-old jewel thief Ralph Emmino's bullet-riddled body was found dumped on Bath Avenue, about a mile from the church, a few days later. No evidence was ever presented linking Emmino to the theft, but, according to the *Brooklyn Eagle*, all of the churches in the diocese united in refusing to afford him a Catholic burial. Every child in my neighborhood knew these stories before we were ten years old.

I never told my parents about receiving tips for serving mass, and with such deception comes the way a child learns the fundamentals of money laundering. If I were to come home with a new pair of Levi's or PF Flyers, my mother would question me about it. But money spent on pizza, movies, and bowling was untraceable. Even small purchases, like 45 rpm records, could disappear into a collection with no raised eyebrows. As long as I remained eager and outwardly grateful for my seventy-cent allowance, life was good. I don't believe this is fundamentally different if you're me or John Gotti or Donald Trump. You just keep adding zeros to the numbers.

The neighborhood as I visualized it revolved on two moving discs, one atop the other. The top one was the picture of society, what you learned in school and read in the newspaper and saw on television. But the lower disc, that was where the action was. That was where the machinery existed that kept the whole thing spinning. That was where tips were generated, and where you pleaded your case when gems were stolen from your church. I knew that there had to be places where both discs were at the same level, but I'd yet to learn what those access points were.

* * *

After grammar school I intentionally chose a high school in Manhattan, wanting to broaden my horizons a little by age fourteen. It was still Catholic—run by Jesuits, in fact—and worse, it was all boys. But it got me out of Brooklyn and into Chelsea every day in the early seventies, only a short walk to the Village and a slightly longer one to *Taxi Driver*-era Times Square. The Jesuits were strict, but they could teach. I'm grateful for that education, and truth be told it kind of spoiled me. From high school I went straight to NYU on a partial scholarship, but the same antsy boredom from grammar school kicked in pretty quickly and I dropped out after a year and a half.

My father had suffered a heart attack, and my mother was working full-time in Midtown, so I took a job across the street from our building, driving car service off the books. The excuse was that I would be nearby to look after my father as he recovered, and after six months or so I'd return to school. Six months at the car service became four years, and as for the return to college, well, that's coming up on forty years as of this writing. But education is where you find it, and I did a lot of growing up bouncing over those potholed streets.

Among our regulars at the car service was a storefront on Thirteenth Avenue called the Wimpy Boys Social Club. We all knew it was a mob hangout, but that was all we knew, at least from my perspective. The owner of the car service had a couple of family members who lived around the fringes of organized crime, yet the rest of our crew were neighborhood guys, no one connected to anybody higher up than the local bookies. The club itself didn't seem like much from the outside, and I remember thinking it looked like a gym. Of course, I never got out of the car to look through the windows.

It was during my car-service days that I first heard the name Greg Scarpa. I honestly don't recall if I associated him with the Wimpy Boys Club, or if I discovered later that it was his operation, but we all knew that we moved through the kingdom the Wimpy Boys ruled.

One night, two of my fellow drivers were sitting in a car at the bus stop outside the storefront, smoking a joint around midnight, when another vehicle raced up, braked violently, and swerved in front of them, pinning their car against the curb. That driver remained in the car and two men jumped out leaving the doors open. One of them had a baseball bat, the other a crowbar. Both of them began with the windshield and shattered every window of the car, while my coworkers screamed in terror and confusion. When all the windows were broken, they got to work on the body, smashing headlights, taillights, then the car itself. As quickly as it began it ended, as though on cue. The men jumped back into their car and the driver roared off.

The whole thing had probably taken fewer than two

minutes. When they recovered enough to move, my friends tentatively got out and surveyed the damage. The car was destroyed, the crowbar still sticking out of the front passenger door, sharp end impaled through the metal. The driver hadn't been injured, and the guy in the passenger seat had a few small cuts in his face from shards of windshield, but was otherwise remarkably unhurt. Each accused the other of having committed some infraction that brought down the wrath of the wiseguys, and each vehemently professed their innocence. No one called the police, and they did not arrive of their own accord.

The next day around midafternoon, the neighborhood hot dog vendor left his aluminum Sabrett cart on the corner and walked the hundred or so feet to our storefront. His name was Joe and I'd known him since I was a small child. He was a nice old guy who spoke very little English, and when he brought his cart home every day, one or two of the kids on the block would run to help him push it up the incline of his driveway. When we got to the top, he would give each of us a free hot dog.

On this day, when he entered the car service, he asked for the driver of the car that had been set upon the night before, by his full name. I was there at the time, and a couple of us must have glanced at the guy because Joe walked over to him. Joe handed him a thick envelope and said slowly, in broken English: "Last night was a mistake. They think you somebody else. They say sorry 'bout that."

Joe smiled at the rest of us, nodded, and walked back up to his cart. Until that moment I would have bet a year's pay that Joe knew less about the workings of the neighborhood than I did. The envelope contained four thousand dollars. The car had been fifteen years old, with a bad transmission, and had cost its owner $650 when he'd bought it a few months earlier.

The driver acted as though he'd hit the lottery; certainly because of the windfall, but much more for learning that people were not looking to harm him over some perceived transgression. His passenger, whose face was already beginning to scab over, was equally relieved, and they immediately set to fighting over the money. The owner of the car service, dispatching that day, served as a mediator. It was ultimately settled that the passenger would get one thousand dollars while the driver kept the other three. By the end of the week he'd secured another run-down relic and was back to work. The balance of the money was gone in bars and the track within a few nights.

During the four years that I worked as a driver, I was aware that I was moving through an alternate universe, suspended in this oddball Brigadoon enclave during the day, and running into Manhattan at night, to CBGB and the Mudd Club. I knew this was temporary and that somehow made it valuable.

Since, as I've said, I had little affinity for higher education, and I was of Irish ancestry living in New York, I took the time-honored route of my forebears into middle-class welfare, otherwise known as civil-service employment. Like everyone, I had grand bohemian aspirations, but at the end of the day that Irish holy trinity of jobs, benefits, and pension is a difficult siren song to ignore if you want to live in relative comfort in this town.

As I've written earlier, I followed my father and most of my uncles into the Transit Authority, working as a night watchman in the train yards for a while. It was all right, and the money was good. But as seniority trumps all in the world of government unions, I found myself working midnight to eight, with Tuesdays and Wednesdays off, and was assured by my foreman that it would take about twelve years to get a steady day tour. So I kept taking every test that came out, probably more than twenty, some for jobs I'd never heard of. Then one day I hit civil-service lotto.

Being a court officer in New York City is a plum government gig. It comes with a decent salary and benefits. It comes with peace officer status, which includes a gun and a badge. You're a little bit like a cop, except you work indoors, Monday to Friday, from nine to five. Mostly you tell criminal defendants where the restrooms are. This, I discovered, was my calling.

It was during my first few years in uniform that I once again came across Greg Scarpa's name. I had access to the computers that ran CRIMS, the New York City criminal-information database, and occasionally needed to use them for work-related information. But, like everyone else, I spent some of my downtime running the names of people I knew. One slow afternoon I ran a dozen or so of my old Regina Pacis classmates, and received two hits. One guy was doing two years on a rape, and the other five-to-ten on gunrunning charges. The rape, sadly, did not surprise me, as that boy had been a problem child when we were seven years old. But the gun charge looked complicated, and when I got the chance I pulled the folder.

That kid, it turned out, followed his older brother down the rabbit hole of low-level organized crime, and had gotten locked up for a half dozen stepping-stone offenses before bringing a couple of machine guns up from somewhere down south and foolishly trying to sell them to a couple of undercover detectives. Although the case resolved itself in federal court, there was enough information in the state file to tie him into the Wimpy Boys crew, and Greg Scarpa was mentioned by name.

For the next several years, though I wasn't seriously paying attention, Scarpa and the Wimpy Boys Social Club would land on my radar in one way or another. And since their territory was my old neighborhood, I always took note of the gamblers and wiseguys passing through, catching last names that I recognized and wondering if they were siblings or children of some of my old friends.

Scarpa himself continued to live the life of the vicious

mob underboss that he was. There were rumors of his connection to multiple murders, and every few years he'd get indicted. In 1991 he survived an attempted hit when two gunmen made a pass at him while his daughter and grandson were driving in the car behind his. He escaped, and being incensed that the attempt had been made around his family, he upped the ante on the ever-present turf wars and bodies began dropping all over South Brooklyn.

In 1992 he shot Lucchese soldier Michael DeRosa in front of DeRosa's house after learning that he'd been threatening Scarpa's son, Greg Jr., over a drug deal gone bad. DeRosa's partner Ronald Moran was there also and returned fire, hitting Scarpa in the eye. So injured, Scarpa drove himself back home, poured a shot of whiskey into the wounded eye socket, and drove himself to the emergency room.

As with all wiseguys, Scarpa eventually ran out of luck and was forced to plead guilty to three murders in 1993. He was sentenced to life in prison. Old, blind in one eye, and suffering from what he told everyone was cancer, he died in the Federal Medical Center in Minnesota in 1994.

And that's when things started to get interesting.

A year after Scarpa's death, during a trial of seven Colombo family mobsters, Carmine Sessa, a former consigliere for the family but now a government witness, revealed that Greg Scarpa had been an FBI informant for over thirty years. Shock waves resonated through the New York world of organized crime, but also law enforcement and local politics. This was a bombshell, but only the tip of the iceberg. The thirty-year relationship took on a sort of Whitey Bulger aspect, as it was alleged that the FBI, and specifically one agent, kept Scarpa propped up and protected. Scarpa would feed the bureau information on his rivals, and in return the government allowed him to operate freely in South Brooklyn.

These revelations were so devastating to federal prosecutors that a total of nineteen murder charges were thrown out or convictions reversed in the government's case against the Orena faction of the Colombo crew. Defense attorneys were able to raise the possibility that the FBI was complicit in Scarpa's war against this branch of the family. A decade or so later, the FBI agent who served as Scarpa's handler during his last active decade would himself be indicted for allegedly aiding Scarpa in the planning of four murders. Those charges were ultimately dismissed.

Along with all the media coverage and courthouse buzz that accompanies mob stories when they break, this one had an added bit of juicy history. The first time I heard it was from a retired FBI agent, in a bar on Court Street.

He told me that back in 1964, as a freshly turned informant, Greg Scarpa's first handler complained in Scarpa's presence about the frustration in the bureau over not being able to locate the bodies of three civil rights workers who'd gone missing over a month earlier in Mississippi. Scarpa more than likely had no familiarity with the case, both Mississippi and civil rights meaning as much to him as Shakespeare's sonnets. But apparently they batted it around and Scarpa finally asked the agent if it would make him look good, so to speak, to locate the bodies. His handler assured him that it would.

The bodies, of course, were those of Andrew Goodman, James Chaney, and Michael Schwerner, the three men murdered in what would become known as the Mississippi Burning case. Scarpa volunteered to help, and not one to pass up the opportunity to show a lady a good time, he brought his young girlfriend Linda Schiro along for the adventure. He arrived with Schiro in Philadelphia, Mississippi, where a locally based FBI agent gave him a gun and helped him rent a late-model Cadillac. The agent also pointed him in the direction of one Lawrence Byrd, a Klansman who owned a television sales and repair shop in Laurel.

Scarpa drove to the store the next afternoon in the large, impressive car, and entered, dressed in his usual top-of-the-line finery. He flashed a lot of green and purchased the most expensive television in the store. He thanked Byrd and told him he'd be back later to pick up the set. When he returned, at closing time, he backed the car up to the door of the store, got out, and opened the trunk. He asked for Byrd's help carrying the set out, and Byrd, still in full flush from the big sale, happily obliged. Scarpa and Byrd brought the television to the car, and carefully placed it on the ground. Scarpa then pitched Byrd headfirst into the trunk and closed it. He drove off to the sound of Byrd's muffled screams, leaving the television at the curb and the door to the store ajar.

He headed to a cabin in the woods, pulled Byrd from the trunk, and dragged him inside. The salesman still had no idea why he'd been abducted. Scarpa beat and pistol-whipped him without speaking, then put the barrel of the revolver down Byrd's throat and asked where the bodies were buried.

Byrd told him.

Scarpa was back in Brooklyn within a few days, and all was right with the world. The FBI located the bodies in the earthen dam where they had been bulldozed after having been shot. Arrests were made, as were headlines, but very little resembling justice came out of that case for more than forty years. Officially, the FBI says a state trooper with ties to several members of the KKK provided the tip. But they don't say it with a lot of confidence. And they certainly don't like to talk about Scarpa at all. At least not on the record.

I was fascinated by the tale, and of course more than a little skeptical. This was alligators-in-the-sewers-level urban legend. There was no way a story like that could be kept quiet for all those years. Except that maybe it had.

Like the best urban legends, the Scarpa Mississippi story kept coming back. I began hearing it in New York City law enforcement circles, and from a couple of district attorneys. There was always some small variation in the tale, but it was essentially as I'd first heard it. Then I heard that it had happened a second time, two years later, in 1966. Scarpa was once again recruited to go down south, this time to break the murder case of an NAACP worker named Vernon Dahmer. This time there were a few more witnesses, including a judge in Laurel named Chet Dillard, who included a reference to the incident in his memoir.

So, did all of this happen?

A handful of retired FBI agents, some of whom worked with Scarpa's handler from the early days, say yes. Judge Dillard says yes. Scarpa's girlfriend of thirty years until his death, mother of two of his children, says yes, and swears she was there the first time. She and Scarpa flew into Mobile, Alabama, the week before the "discovery" of the three buried civil rights workers. Seems an unlikely vacation spot for a romantic weekend in 1964.

I thought about all of this on Martin Luther King Jr. Day this year. Is it important? Should we incorporate Greg Scarpa into folk songs as a hero of the movement? Abraham, Martin, and Greg?

I often wonder what Scarpa himself would have made

of those trips. He could not have been more out of place if he'd been dropped in Beijing. There had to be a comedic aspect. On some level, it's *My Cousin Vinny* directed by Quentin Tarantino. It's easy to imagine Scarpa's contempt for the Klan and their operation in the South back then. A shadow empire, controlling hundreds of miles and millions of people through intimidation and brutality, and nobody was making a fucking nickel. How that must have galled him. A syndicate that dealt in violence without profit must have seemed stupid to the point of indecency.

Scarpa was a man very comfortable with those revolving discs I mentioned earlier. As a kid, I envisioned them propelling the neighborhood, but Scarpa knew that they moved the whole country, maybe the whole world. He'd acquainted himself with all the access points and stepped on and off in his own life with ease, and always to his personal benefit.

Upping the ante on irony is the fact that toward the end of his life, while Scarpa told everyone that he was suffering from cancer, he was actually dying of AIDS. He'd undergone surgery a few years prior for stomach ulcers, and, fearing that he might get the blood of a Black person in the transfusion, ordered all of his crew who were of compatible type to donate. One of those men, Paul Mele, was a weight lifter who had been shooting steroids, and had contracted the disease by sharing needles.

* * *

I recently went back to Regina Pacis for the first time in many years. The grand staircase leading up to the main entrance of the church seemed much smaller than my childhood recollection, but honestly, not much else had changed. The school is closed now, so I don't know where the influx of altar boys comes from, if indeed they are still around. When I'd begun, masses were said in English and Italian. They still are, but now, every Sunday, there's also a service in Spanish and one in Chinese. I stood in front of the altar where I'd served mass, inhaled the never-forgotten scents of candle wax, incense, and boredom, genuflected to Jesus and Joe Profaci, and left.

I asked one of my childhood friends if he recalled Father Sforza, wondering if I'd remembered the name correctly. We argued about the spelling, so I googled him. I'd been correct, it was Sforza, with no apostrophe. That was when I also learned that he is listed on the database of Catholic priests in the Diocese of Brooklyn accused of child sex abuse. The allegations stem from his time at Regina Pacis in the late 1960s, when I was an altar boy there. I'd had no idea. I'd been a fairly social kid from an intact family, so I guess I wasn't a target. I was plucky enough to insist that I could perform those duties at a younger age. Maybe that made me a little too assertive. It also resulted in the service age being lowered to eight years old, which hasn't been lost on me.

Father Sforza was another player who understood the

moving discs, stepping back and forth between the world of authority and artifice, and the world where that authority gave him the power to indulge his compulsions.

I've spent a lifetime watching those discs, and I'm no closer to understanding their institutional momentum than when I was a child. We fight about where transgender people should be allowed to urinate, then send our children to houses of worship where clergy sexually abuse them. We support law enforcement, who then utilize the services of people they should be arresting, psychotic killers from the depths of the underworld. In thirty years in the criminal justice system, I watched dozens of people who were factually guilty of murder walk through the doors because of some legal technicality, or simply bad police or prosecutorial work. They now ride the subways with us; we jostle each other at newsstands. In one instance, one was my waiter in a restaurant in Chelsea.

Who are the heroes?

Who are the monsters?

I'm tipping a glass today to Martin Luther King Jr., and one to Greg Scarpa. I'm not a religious man, but I'll hedge my bets enough to toast looking up for the first, down for the second.

Excited Utterances

I remember exactly where I was standing and what I was doing the first time I heard a 710.30(1)(a) statement, but then, who doesn't? I was a brand-new, wet-behind-the-ears court officer in the arraignment part of Brooklyn Criminal Court in the bad old 1980s. I was the bridgeman, the officer who stands in front of the judge's bench, calls the case into the record, hands the judge the pertinent paperwork, and gets out of the way. It's just like *Law & Order*, except louder and with physically unattractive defendants. It was my first case, and I announced it with confidence, then prepared the next docket while the key players discussed the fate of the accused. After preliminary conversation and a plea of not guilty, the judge turned to the rail-thin blond waif of an assistant district attorney.

"Motions?" he asked.

"Seven-ten-thirty-one-a," she responded.

"Go ahead."

"Go fuck yourself," she said, in an absolutely flat, professional tone.

"Anything else?"

"No, Your Honor."

"Bail is set at one thousand dollars, cash or bond," he said. "Next case."

He tossed the court papers into the wire basket of finished work and looked at me expectantly. I glanced between him and the ADA, who was already reviewing a new folder, unsure what to do.

"Officer," he prompted.

I picked up the next docket, called it in, less confidently this time, and stepped back.

It took me perhaps a half dozen cases before I realized that 710.30(1)(a) statements were direct quotes from defendants, usually made spontaneously at the time of their arrest. It was therefore not unusual that mixed in with the ubiquitous *that's not my gun* and *what weed?* would be the occasional *go fuck yourself* or *take these cuffs off and I'll kick your ass*. They are basically anything that gets blurted out during the arrest process. Arraignment in New York City Criminal Court is supposed to be conducted within twenty-four hours of arrest. In an effort to keep to that schedule, the processing of cases goes on from nine o'clock in the morning until midnight every day of the year in Brooklyn at 120 Schermerhorn Street, just down the block from all of the shiny new condos and hotels being raised downtown.

Over the course of the three years that I worked in uniform, I listened to hundreds of 710.30(1)(a) statements, and came to view them as windows on the unrestrained id.

They can be chilling, as in the case of a man caught in Sunset Park discarding the bloody remains of his pit bull: *He farted so I stabbed him.*

They can be heartbreaking, as when a man in East New York is arrested for robbery: *I'm sorry. I was hungry. I needed the money. I got the blade on me too.*

They can be embarrassing, as in a domestic-violence case out of East Flatbush, when a defense attorney has just told the judge that the court needs to take into account the social mores of other cultures: *She doesn't have my lunch ready for me when I go to work. I want her to do all the cleaning in the house. Today, I told her to make me breakfast, and when I went downstairs she hadn't made me breakfast. That's how it started.*

And, of course, they can be hilarious. After all, if you can't occasionally find humor in someone else's misdeeds, you have no business calling yourself a New Yorker. My personal favorite was the young man arrested exiting the basement of an apartment building in Crown Heights where every washing machine and dryer in the laundry room had been vandalized. He was carrying a screwdriver, a hammer, and a pillowcase containing 250 quarters: *Those are mine, I'm on my way to a Pac-Man tournament. The tools are to fix the machines.*

This parade of tragedy and comedy occurs for fifteen hours a day, seven days a week. And though the poor and anonymous comprise the majority of cases, every demographic makes an appearance. I have witnessed the arraignments of lawyers and doctors, police officers and priests, a former Major League Baseball player and a judge. They are not the worst of humanity, but what they share is the airing of their worst behavior. The criminal justice system, by mandating long ago that these proceedings be open to the public, invented reality television without the TV, live and unscripted.

So if the Real Housewives of Wherever's latest catfight is wearing thin, come to a place where the term "survivor" is more apropos than what you've been watching. Come down to any of the criminal courthouses. Not supreme court, regular criminal court, where the nobodies stay but even the superstars make that initial appearance. Enter through the smoke-darkened revolving doors, their broken glass long ago replaced with Plexiglas. Pass through the magnetometers and be searched for weapons, and then have a seat in one of the pews scored with decades of carved initials and expletives. There's a new show every three minutes.

Welcome to reality theater.

PIMPS AND HOES

Some years back I went down to Atlantic City with a couple of friends for what we'd dubbed a "mental health weekend." A little gambling, too much alcohol, and rich food, just three guys horsing around. About an hour after we'd arrived, one of my buddies got lucky and won fifteen hundred dollars on a fifty-cent slot machine. We stuck five hundred dollars in his shoe, declared a moratorium on betting, and set about spending the remaining thousand over the next eighteen hours. It was Halloween weekend, and the casino at which we were staying, the Borgata, was throwing a pimps-and-hoes party. We'd had no prior knowledge of the event, and since we hadn't anticipated a windfall, we were woefully ill prepared for any sort of costume affair, unless the theme was middle-aged assholes. But we attended, and mingled with a festive group that was taking this game very seriously. Provocatively clad women in fetish outfits hung on to the arms of white guys done up like Superfly, complete with feathered hats and canes. A woman in her thirties, who was dressed like a schoolgirl in a short plaid skirt, saddle shoes, and pigtails, approached me at the bar and asked why I wasn't in costume.

"Oh, I'm in costume," I said.

"Really?" she said. "What are you?"

"I'm a pimp."

"Pimps don't look like that."

"Sadly, this is exactly what they look like."

I smiled and she moved off quickly.

Pimps are people who put prostitutes to work and take a cut of their earnings. Decked out in my most fly khakis and Florsheims, I was the only real pimp in the room.

I had started working as a court officer in Brooklyn Criminal Court in the summer of 1983. I'd been born and raised in Brooklyn, and I've still never lived anywhere else. At the time, I considered myself a reasonably savvy New Yorker, having come of age here in the 1970s. I'd gone to high school on 16th Street in Chelsea, and the streetwalkers on Lexington Avenue would proposition and taunt me and my friends as we made our way to the subway station after school. They'd tease us with offers of student discounts, and pull at our clothes when we went by, and as fourteen-year-old boys we were nervous and thrilled.

It was a dramatically different experience eleven years later when I first saw prostitutes brought before the court for arraignment. These were Brooklyn hookers. Brooklyn hookers in the 1980s. They looked tired, defiant, and addled. They wore sweatshirts and torn jeans and sneakers. They in no way resembled the exotic women of *Taxi Driver*–era Manhattan. Brooklyn was a world away from Manhattan back then, and crack had arrived.

The first six or seven cases were called so quickly that it took me a few moments to realize that pleas had been taken and sentences imposed. But they all had one thing in common. Every case was resolved with the imposition of a fine. No jail time, no community service. I was instructed to escort the women, along with their paperwork, to the cashier's office, and remain with them until their names were called and the fines paid. Then they were free to leave, and I returned to the courtroom. This was repeated four or five times on my first day of work, and by the end of my shift, over two dozen women had been arraigned, sentenced, and released.

The following week, I bumped into the arraignment ADA in Callahan's, a bar on Remsen Street, conveniently located within three blocks of the criminal, civil, and family courts, as well as the district attorney's office and Legal Aid Society. Court officers, clerks, and lawyers converged there most nights, especially toward the end of the week. I asked him why the prostitution cases were disposed of with fines instead of jail time.

"No prost is gonna plead out to jail time," he said. "They'd fight the cases, clog the system. We'd never get through the day."

"But they're hookers," I said, "and we're fining them. Do you think they're going to get jobs as office temps to pay those fines?"

"It's small potatoes. You have to pick your fights. Does it bother you?"

"I don't know," I said honestly, "I just never saw myself as a pimp."

Two weeks into the new job, I was with another rookie officer early in the morning, setting up an empty courtroom, when we heard a loud pounding on the wall that made the hanging calendar jump. At the same time someone began screaming. We ran out into the hallway and saw a man throttling a woman and repeatedly slamming her head against the wall. My partner and I pulled him off and took him down to the floor. As we restrained him, discovering for the first time how difficult it is to handcuff someone who does not want to be handcuffed, he kept yelling at us. His cry was like a mantra, repeated over and over again, part complaint, part instruction: "She's my wife." That was all he said. No explanation, no litany of her offenses against him, not even the usual denial of the act. Just, "She's my wife."

By the time we had him cuffed and standing, the

woman, still leaning on the wall, began pleading that we not arrest him. We brought him downstairs to the captain's office and placed him in the small holding area with two other men who'd been arrested in the building that day, awaiting transportation to Central Booking. As I was leaving, one of the men asked the new guy why he was there.

"Hitting my wife," he said.

"No shit?" the other guy said, shaking his head. "Damn, they lock you up now for hittin' your own woman."

I went back to work, letting people with more experience sort out the mess. The woman was still arguing with my captain. Later in the day we learned that the man had been released.

I no longer felt like a savvy New Yorker. It was as if my whole life to this point had been lived in some sort of protective bubble. I was like one of the guys from the suburbs, the officers whom, even as a rookie, I openly mocked for their naivete. The really tough part, not just for me but for my partner as well, was trying to decide whether that woman was better off for having interacted with us. If we hadn't been there, would her husband have seriously injured her? Might he have killed her? Or would he have stopped, as I'm sure had happened numerous times before, when his rage was spent? We'd certainly made him angrier. What happened when they got home? I never even learned why they'd been in court.

I'd had no illusions about going into this line of work

to fight crime. I was an outer-borough working-class white kid with a high school diploma and no appetite for higher education. I came to this gig because it had most of the benefits of the police department, but you worked indoors and got weekends off. Still, I'd always assumed that if I went through the motions and was competent, life would be better at the end of the day, or at least no worse. Now I wasn't sure.

After about a month, I rotated into a trial part and worked my first jury case. It was a rape trial. The defendant was accused of acting in concert with an unapprehended partner in abducting a young woman and forcing her into his van late at night in the Wall Street area. They drove to a deserted part of East New York, took turns assaulting her, and left her in a vacant lot. She was an office worker who routinely worked from four p.m. to midnight then took the subway home to Queens. She was twenty-three, Haitian, and an evangelical Christian who read her Bible during her commute. Her accused attacker was a Brooklyn native with three prior convictions for selling marijuana in the same part of lower Manhattan from which she'd been abducted.

The defense attorney was pretty good; the ADA was not. The defendant didn't take the stand, the woman's sexual history was trotted out, and the judge ruled that the marijuana convictions would prejudice the jury, so there was nothing admitted that put the defendant regularly in the vicinity. The procedural details argued between the lawyers and the judge, before and during the trial, and outside the jury's presence, made it clear that all parties acknowledged the defendant's factual guilt. The jury deliberated for a few hours before acquitting him of all charges except resisting arrest, a misdemeanor for which he was fined and sentenced to probation.

After the trial, both attorneys asked if jurors would talk to them about the case and why they voted the way they did. I came to learn that this was pretty standard; jurors usually agreed to be interviewed. It was very informal, conducted out in the hall, all parties standing around chatting with their coats on. I was assigned to stand with them until they were done, and heard one of the last jurors, an elderly woman dressed in an old but immaculate fake fur coat, speak to the ADA. He asked whether she believed that the defendant was innocent, or simply that his guilt hadn't been proven beyond a reasonable doubt.

"Well," she said, "I'm pretty sure he done it, but she wasn't a virgin, so I can't see putting the boy away."

I took him upstairs to pay his fine.

I wasn't the only rookie trying to make sense of the system. A few months into the job, I was working as bridgeman in arraignments, organizing the cases and calling them into the record, when a new judge began her first day. On this particular day there had been another prostitution sweep, in Coney Island. Two or three pimps were in the audience, and I held the cases until their regular attorney arrived.

One aspect of criminal court that surprised me was how many lawyers were specialists, and how many were on retainer. They were characters right out of central casting, if Fellini were making a movie from a Damon Runyon novel. The gambler's attorney was a gentleman who looked like Tarzan. He had a perennially baked-in tan that turned orange in winter, and shoulder-length blond hair. He wore thousand-dollar suits and Gucci loafers. The weed guy was tall and thin and looked like Dracula. In fact, we called him the Count. He dressed exclusively in funereal black and conducted all his business from the shoeshine stand in the lobby. The stand had three seats, and the Count would sit in the left corner and place his clients in the center to interview them. If someone wanted a shine they sat on the right. Joe, the shoeshine attendant, was well into his eighties and had been working there for forty years. He had a locker and a landline. The Count kept a locker next to Joe's and used Joe's phone. I don't know if he actually maintained an office, but I know he supplemented the shiner's income. And he was in the Rolodex of every ganja dealer in Brooklyn. If someone was going to be arraigned for a substantial amount of weed, the Count would be there.

The lawyer who stood up on all the prostitution cases was short and obese with a bad toupee, but he always dressed impeccably and, with his girth, must have had his suits custom-made. I could not swear that he was on the payroll of every pimp in Brooklyn, but I never saw another retained attorney stand up for a soliciting charge.

On this day, with a brand-new judge taking the bench, I lined up the first ten or twelve prostitution cases and began calling them. After I read the charges on the first case, the ADA made the standard offer of a plea to disorderly conduct and a hundred-dollar fine. The defense attorney accepted, and I'd already started noting the folder when the judge spoke.

"No," she said, "that plea is not acceptable to the court. I think five days is in order."

"Your Honor," the attorney said, "these cases are usually resolved with a fine."

"This is her sixteenth arrest for soliciting, Counselor. I don't think the fines are working."

One of the pimps leaned over the rail and whispered to the attorney, who then suggested to the judge that the fine be doubled.

"No," the judge said. "Five days or she can go to trial, and we'll discuss bail conditions."

The pimps were buzzing and the obese lawyer began to look ill. He argued some more but got nowhere. Ultimately, the judge pointed out that five days wasn't so bad. She'd be released after three, that being the standard two-thirds of the sentence, and with credit for the day she'd spent being processed it would mean that she would only serve two more. The girl took it. The pimps were furious. Fine money they could replace, the girl would just have to work that much harder, but losing a revenue stream set a bad precedent.

The next two cases went the same way, yet on the fourth, the defendant had a meltdown. Her lawyer tried to explain what was happening, but she erupted in rage.

"I don't want no time!" she yelled at him. "I want a fuckin' fine. Larry," she called into the audience, "you get me a fine."

Her pimp did not seem eager to be identified and left the courtroom. The lawyers and the judge began negotiating, then the defendant had a second outburst. "Fuck this shit, get me another judge, I want another judge! Get me a judge that knows how to sentence prosts."

After that tirade the defendant was removed from the courtroom. Her attorney suggested to the court that she might be unstable.

"Counselor," the judge replied, "I would be more than happy to order a thirty-day in-house psychiatric exam, if you think your client might benefit from it. Or she can be held in contempt for ten days. Or, she can apologize to the court and take the five-day sentence."

The attorney went back to confer with his client, returned with her, and guided her through her apology. She got the five days. So did every other hooker who came through arraignments. It seemed there was a new sheriff in town. When I returned to work the next day I learned the judge had been reassigned. Standard rotation through arraignments was a week. That judge did not rotate back into the arraignment part during the time I worked there in uniform.

I spent three years as an officer before being promoted to court clerk. It seemed like a sensible career move. Being a clerk was less exciting, but rolling around on the floor with wife beaters wasn't something I'd want to be doing when I was in my forties. As a clerk, I worked a trial part devoted exclusively to crack cocaine cases for three months, then did a year in housing court, and then I was transferred into the job that would carry me through the rest of my career. I was assigned to the cashier's office.

The irony of this move wasn't lost on me. I'd now eliminated the middleman and moved up the pimp food chain. That transition, although I was now a step removed from the actual machinery of the courtroom, seemed to put me in more visceral contact with criminal defendants. I came to realize that most of them were just life's losers: people dealt a bad hand or addled by addiction. But among these, and maybe because of the sheer number of life's losers, the bad guys stood out.

I'd gotten used to the fact that we essentially tax commercial sex, in the same way that we tax illegal gambling and possession of marijuana. It seemed like you could do business in this town as long as you paid the freight. But now I was collecting money from rapists. I was collecting money from pedophiles. In two cases, I collected money from people convicted of distributing child pornography through the mail. Those cases involved large fines, usually around five thousand dollars. The defendant in one instance had made arrangements with the court to pay it off at a hundred dollars per month, so I dealt with him for over four years. He became one of my regulars, and used to initiate conversations about sports while he stood at the window. Here's the creepy part: sometimes I would respond.

There was something about the mercantile nature of these relationships and their ongoing duration that made them feel somehow more than professional. The interactions sometimes became cordial. Although sexual offenses represented a small percentage of the volume of work that passed through my office, sex offender registry fee cases probably averaged a little over a dozen per month. I was in the business of rape. If a case was disposed of in a single payment, then it wasn't uncommon for me not to know the details of the crime until after the defendant had left, if I even bothered to look at them at all. But we recorded the charges, and I knew the penal law codes, so I was aware of the nature of each crime.

We have all learned that serial killers, for the most part, don't look like Hannibal Lecter. More often, they look like Don Knotts. Well, sex offenders look like all of us. From Hasidic Jews to sixty-year-old Black women, I saw no more diversely represented demographic among the criminal public than those convicted of sexual violence.

Most defendants did not pay in full, and that meant several adjournments, and several more visits. When that happened I'd often look at the folder to see what the defendant had done. Sometimes I wished I hadn't. One well-dressed guy with an anachronistic pencil mustache came up to the window with a young girl holding his arm and looking at him adoringly. He made a fifty-dollar partial payment on his thousand-dollar fine and received an adjournment to return the following month. Before leaving, he gestured with his chin toward the very thick case folder on the counter in front of me.

"See that?" he said to her. "That's all about me. I told you I was a bad guy."

She smiled sweetly and they walked out. When I examined his file I learned that beyond the twenty or so prior arrests, the present conviction was for forcing himself into the apartment of an ex-girlfriend, raping her, and killing her dog. He'd taken a felony plea, his first, and received six months' jail time and five years' probation.

I tried to keep my exchanges with offenders brief, but sometimes, before I realized it, I'd be lured into a kind of genuine conversation. When that happens with a gambler or burglar you don't really think about it, but when it happens with a sexual predator it stays with you, most obviously because it's unwelcome contact, unpleasant on its face. But, on a deeper level, you feel like someone has breached your personal security, and you come to realize how easily that security can be breached, and you think about the people who have experienced that at the hands of this defendant, and it makes you frightened and sad.

Then you tell them to have a nice day and they leave, and you wonder for a while what they might do that night, and to whom. Then you call the next case.

I wasn't by any means a rookie anymore. I'd settled into this career and made a sort of uneasy peace with that decision. But if taking money from prostitutes to let them go back to work made me a pimp, then what the fuck did taking money from rapists and watching them walk out the door make me? I spent a lot of years trying to figure that out. Truth be told, I'm still trying.

The phases I went through over the course of my career probably mirrored those of most men and women in law enforcement or other criminal justice jobs. The first thing that changes is your point of reference.

I grew up Irish Catholic, and in my community, churches and the parish often represented neighborhoods. You didn't live in Park Slope; you either lived in Holy Name or Saint Saviour. After starting my career, precincts replaced that perspective. They were the identifiers among my coworkers, and we all quickly learned them and their boundaries. When someone told me conversationally where they lived, I'd flash on that precinct and its stats. I'd wonder if the person I was speaking to knew what went on in their neighborhood. I'd remember specific crimes.

There was the gun phase. I was required to wear a firearm at work, but I'd initially decided that I probably wouldn't carry one when off duty. Within six months I wore it any time I left the house. The gun phase ended abruptly when a girl I was dating remarked that she found it unsettling that I put it on to take out the trash. A part of me wanted to tell her about a victim I'd seen who was robbed and beaten on his own stoop while taking out the trash, but fortunately, another part of me realized that, although it was the truth, it didn't mean that wearing a gun to take out your garbage wasn't crazy. I stopped carrying and never missed it.

There is a danger of seeing individuals on the street and automatically assessing them as predators, or prey. If you fall into that, even a little, it can be soul deadening. I believe that it accounts for the large number of people in law enforcement who move as far from the cities that they work in as they can, sometimes enduring extraordinary commutes to work. It accounts for them becoming overly protective of friends and family. And it explains the shell that they put in place, the pose of gruff indifference to human suffering, because the suffering isn't going away, and twenty to thirty years is a long time to deal with it five days a week.

When crime is commoditized it becomes a commodity.

And those involved in it, as perpetrators or victims, become product. If you don't believe that, just look at the private prison industry in this country. Whatever your political inclination, I've yet to see a convincing argument since the abolition of slavery that it is constitutionally permitted to imprison human beings for profit.

But even on a municipal level, the endless days and constant repetitive exposure to antisocial behavior breeds a level of callousness born of self-preservation. It is present in most court officers and clerks just as it is in most cops. But it also affects the attorneys, both prosecutors and defense counsel, and judges. It's there in the journalists assigned to cover courthouse proceedings. The most horrific of crimes, after the dead have been buried and the blood is washed away, are ultimately processed in a building that looks a lot like an insurance company. Folders are notated, fees and fines imposed and collected, victims, if they have survived, return home to recover and rebuild lives, and people who commit monstrous acts either go to jail or don't, depending upon the veracity of witnesses, acuity of counsel, or attention span of a jury.

One of the most egregious examples of this sort of callousness that I ever encountered occurred while I was standing outside my building at lunchtime, waiting for a friend. A lengthy, awful trial had recently concluded, and two defendants had just been sentenced to life imprisonment for the kidnapping, rape, and murder of a young woman. They were textbook monsters. They tortured her for three days before killing her with a hammer. Soon after, they abducted and raped another girl who subsequently managed to get away and contact the police. During their trial, they attempted to escape the courthouse, wielding makeshift Plexiglas knives, stabbing one of their own lawyers, and trying to grab a court officer's gun. As for the girl's death, at sentencing one of them stated, "We did it for fun."

The same day in a different courtroom, another rape and murder case was just beginning, this one much more high profile. The victim was from a wealthy family, had lived on the Upper West Side of Manhattan, and was in graduate school.

The mother of the first victim had attended the sentencing of her daughter's killers, and while I was standing outside, she emerged from the building. Dozens of reporters and cameramen surrounded her, calling out questions and requests for comments. She composed herself, and then began to speak. She spoke about her relief that the verdict had been what it was, but she also aired her grievances about the police and the media. She expressed frustration and anger over the difficulty her family had experienced in getting anyone interested in her daughter's disappearance.

While she was speaking, the family of the other murder victim emerged from the building. At once, most of the press abandoned the first grieving mother and rushed to the second, cameras and microphones jostling as they scurried across the plaza. The mother of the first victim was startled, and faltered for a moment, then finished speaking to the two or three reporters who hadn't fled. The moment she stopped they too departed, chasing their colleagues who were disappearing around the corner. Two stories needed to be covered. What were the odds that the opportunity for quotes on two rape and murder cases would come simultaneously? Everyone's just doing their job. But watching that woman stand there alone is something I will never forget.

The demographics of New York changed radically during my years in the system, and those changes were reflected in the criminal community. Some of them are pretty meaningless, one ethnic group supplanting another in certain neighborhoods. Swapping Italian drug dealers for Asians in Bensonhurst, Hispanic loan sharks for Russians in Williamsburg and Bushwick. Watching the South Brooklyn gamblers migrate to Staten Island, as it becomes the new old Brooklyn.

Other changes are more disturbing. The desiccated crack whores of the eighties and nineties, who had replaced the sassy flamboyant streetwalkers of the seventies, have now also been replaced. The prostitutes that come through today are mostly Russian and Asian. They are usually silent, and keep their eyes downcast. They speak little or no English. They come in groups of three or four, often accompanied by small, neatly dressed men who stand nearby as they pay, then they all leave together.

The broken-windows policy implemented nearly twenty years ago targeted the commercial sex trade, and along with removing panhandlers and squeegee guys at busy intersections, it has improved the quality of life in many parts of the city. But the squeegee guys aren't still cleaning windshields with their dirty rags indoors. Panhandlers aren't begging in their living rooms. Yet sex workers are still working, they have just been driven further underground. That, combined with the influx of new immigrant groups and their attendant vulnerabilities, has resulted in the human trafficking nightmare that has largely replaced more traditional vice networks. If it was once true that most prostitutes were victims of their own bad choices, lack of options, or addiction, now many are genuinely held in slavery.

It would be unfair not to acknowledge that there has been progress. There are now integrated domestic violence courts in New York City and larger metropolitan areas upstate. They track cases that cross the lines from criminal- to family-court matters, so that real resolution can sometimes occur. In Queens, a visionary judge initiated a prostitution diversion court, to treat prostitutes as victims, and where possible to get them away from traffickers. But it is such small change against such a vast landscape, and on my last day at work we were still collecting money from people waiting in line as though they were at a supermarket, alternating drunk drivers and date rapists.

I don't know a better way to state this, but for all the gentrification of this city and the attendant drop in crime, for all the advancements of the last thirty years in outreach programs and counseling, all we've really accomplished is to render the unpalatable invisible. The world through which vulnerable women move seems meaner than ever.

I'm retired now, but of course I'm still part of the system. I vote and pay taxes. I even serve on jury duty in the buildings where I once worked. And as part of the system I still feel complicit. It's a system that often does good and administers justice, but that too often processes people as product—rapists and car thieves, pedophiles and unlicensed drivers, pimps and other predators as though they were shoplifters. Sometimes the victims within the crimes get convicted and fined too, and disappear into the depths of that criminal invisibility. And the system still generates revenue indiscriminately, from both organized vice and individual psychotic acts.

So, at the end of the day, I'm still a pimp. And so are you.

Acknowledgments

I'd like to thank the crew at Akashic Books—Johanna Ingalls, Aaron Petrovich, Susannah Lawrence, Alex Verdan, Ibrahim Ahmad, and Sohrab Habibion—who have labored for years to make me look much smarter than I am.

Very special thanks are due to Kaylie Jones and Johnny Temple, each of whom has changed my life, and to Renette Zimmerly, who saved it.

Stories from this collection have appeared in the following publications: "Scared Rabbit" in *New Orleans Noir*, Akashic Books; "Seven Eleven" in *Long Island Noir*, Akashic Books; "Opening Day" in *The Subway Chronicles*, Penguin Books; "Surfing the Crimewave" (under the title "New York State of Crime") in *New York Calling*, Reaktion Books UK, University of Chicago Press US; "Excited Utterances" (in slightly altered form and under the title "Reality Television Without the TV") in *A Public Space Literary Supplement to the ABA*; "When All This Was Bay Ridge" in *Brooklyn Noir* and *USA Noir*, Akashic Books, and *Best American Mystery Stories 2005*, Houghton Mifflin Company. "Indigenous" was recorded with the band Cinema Cinema.

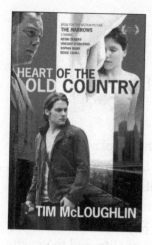